Once

STAND-ALONE NOVEL

A Western Historical Adventure Book

by

Zachary McCrae

RUBEDIA
PUBLISHING

Disclaimer & Copyright

This is a work of fiction. Names, characters, places, and incidents are either products of the author's imagination or are used fictitiously. Any resemblance to actual events, locales, or persons, living or dead, is entirely coincidental.

Copyright © 2025 by Zachary McCrae

All Rights Reserved.

No part of this book may be reproduced, duplicated, transmitted, or recorded in any form—electronic or printed—without the prior written permission of the publisher. Unauthorized storage or distribution of this document is strictly prohibited.

Table of Contents

Once a Lawman 1
   Disclaimer & Copyright 2
   Table of Contents 3
   Letter from Zachary McCrae 5
Prologue 6
Chapter One 11
Chapter Two 18
Chapter Three 25
Chapter Four 30
Chapter Five 39
Chapter Six 47
Chapter Seven 53
Chapter Eight 61
Chapter Nine 69
Chapter Ten 75
Chapter Eleven 81
Chapter Twelve 87
Chapter Thirteen 94
Chapter Fourteen 101
Chapter Fifteen 107
Chapter Sixteen 114
Chapter Seventeen 121
Chapter Eighteen 128
Chapter Nineteen 137

Chapter Twenty 143
Chapter Twenty-One 152
Chapter Twenty-Two 159
Chapter Twenty-Three 168
Chapter Twenty-Four 173
Chapter Twenty-Five 176
Chapter Twenty-Six 184
Chapter Twenty-Seven 191
Chapter Twenty-Eight 196
Chapter Twenty-Nine 203
Chapter Thirty 209
Chapter Thirty-One 214
Chapter Thirty-Two 221
Chapter Thirty-Three 225
Epilogue 230
  Also by Zachary McCrae 235

Letter from Zachary McCrae

I'm a man who loves plain things: a cup of strong coffee in the morning, a good book at noon, and my wife's embrace at night.

I want to write stories that take you by the hand and show you what it meant to be someone who tried to make ends meet and find their own way in the 19th-century United States. I've been this someone for a long time in my life, always looking for my next gig after my parents' sudden death, always finding new friends, but somehow not being able to stick with 'em. It's easy to find quantity in your life, but what about quality?

At the age of 50, and after my baby boy, Jeb, and my sweet daughter, Janette, went away to study East, with my sweet wife, Mrs. Maryanne McCrae, we moved back to my hometown and my dad's ranch close to the Rockies. After a series of health issues that have brought me even closer to our Lord, I've officially started writing those stories I always loved to read.

I'm tending my land and animals now with the help of Maryanne, and I'm grateful for each day I get to walk in this world we call Earth. As the saying goes, "Nature gave us all something to fall back on, and sooner or later we all land flat on it," so I want to take care of it just the way it has taken care of my dad and mom, and my cousins.

My adventure stories are my legacy to my children and to all of the readers who will honor me by following my work. God bless you and your families and our land! Thank you.

Stay safe but adventurous,

Zachary McCrae

Prologue

Western Nebraska, 1870

You won't get away this time.

Nate Holt shifted in the saddle, leather creaking beneath him. Henry, his buckskin gelding, tossed his head, picking up on the tension in Nate's grip. The reins were tight, just like Nate's jaw.

A glint off the saddle buckle caught his eye, just enough reflection to glimpse the face beneath his hat's brim. Weathered skin, creased by too many days in the saddle. Nut-brown beard, trimmed neatly. Eyes, sharp and blue as a prairie lake.

Not too bad for an old, weather-beaten sheriff.

Nate often felt older than the hills, his dogged determination to seek justice aging him beyond his near forty years on this earth.

Now, after three years, twelve seasons, Owen Pike was trapped like a rattlesnake in a barrel.

I've got you this time.

Wind stirred, whispering through the grass as if anticipating the coming battle. Nate adjusted his hat, the brim cracked and sun-faded, and squinted west. The setting sun bled red across the horizon, ready to drop into night.

Barrett Rivers, his deputy, rode up beside him, rifle resting casually across his lap, eyes sharp above a day's growth of beard. "You feel it?" he murmured. "Like we almost got him?"

"He's close. I can almost smell him."

Behind them, six men rode in silence, a posse of deputies, trackers, and one ex-scout, Royce Tate, who could read a trail like an Apache.

For three years, they'd been chasing Owen Pike, the Coyote Clan's ruthless leader, through badlands and blizzards, across state lines, and into the belly of outlaw country. Each time they'd been close, Pike had slipped through their fingers like smoke. But not today.

Today, they had him cornered in a box canyon.

Today, he won't escape.

Nate raised a hand, and his men guided their horses closer. "We're near the ridge," he said decisively. "He's holed up in that canyon up ahead. We spotted smoke last night. No movement since dawn."

Nate's heart thudded against his ribs, raw fear sent his breath pulsing in his throat. "He's still in there."

"And he's not alone," Barrett added. "His gang's getting ready to move. We'll wait for your signal, Nate. I figure you're aiming for Pike, so we'll handle the rest—right, fellas?"

Murmurs of agreement rippled through the posse.

Nate's fingers brushed the grip of his Colt. He hadn't drawn it in months. Most of the time, he didn't need to—his reputation as sheriff of Niobrara did the talking for him—but today, he had a feeling he would.

"Still carrying that old piece?" Royce Tate's glance flicked to the weapon, a grin spreading over his chapped lips. "You've had that Colt since God booted Adam from Eden. Reckon you can fire it?"

A brief smile crossed Nate's face. "Only when I mean business."

They dismounted quietly, tying their horses behind a thicket of scrub oak. The canyon mouth yawned ahead, flanked by jagged rock and deep shadow. Moving furtively, the posse spread out, climbing the rugged stone cliffs.

Nate crouched beside Barrett, peering through a bushy tangle of sagebrush. Below, the Coyote Clan moved like ants, packing saddlebags, checking rifles, laughing like they hadn't a care in the world.

"They think they're safe," Barrett muttered, a grim smile playing across his lips.

Nate's jaw tightened. "Let's show 'em otherwise." He raised two fingers and thrust them forward. The posse began to circle the canyon from both sides.

Nate waited, steadying his breathing, eyes fixed on Owen Pike. He'd spent hours analyzing Pike, trying to understand the motives of a man who'd devoted his life to thievery, indifferent to how many bodies he left behind. In the end, though, nothing could justify such evil.

Shaking off his musings, Nate raised his hand.

Thunder erupted as his men opened fire, shattering the stillness. The canyon echoed with gunfire as bullets tore through the dry air, ricocheting off stone and splintering scrub. Pike's gang, once confident in their isolation, scrambled like cornered rats.

Smoke curled from the muzzle of Nate's Colt as he ducked behind a jagged outcrop, then twisted to peer into the bedlam. A gray haze formed as the scurrying outlaws kicked up dust in desperate retreat.

Barrett's voice rang out above the din. "Push forward! Don't let 'em escape!"

As the posse fanned out, rifles cracking rhythmically, Nate flanked left, weaving between boulders and mesquite. He spotted a bandit crouched behind a fallen log, frantically reloading.

Nate didn't hesitate; he fired, and the man slumped forward with a choked cry.

From the ridge, another outlaw sent rounds whistling past Nate's head. He dove, rolled, and came up firing. The man dropped his rifle and tumbled backward, disappearing into the brush.

Pike barked hoarse orders from the center of the camp. "Hold your ground, you dag! Keep shooting!"

A few men obeyed, dragging crates and barrels into a makeshift barricade. One lit a stick of dynamite, hurling it toward the advancing posse. It landed short, exploding in a shower of dirt and flame. Horses reared and men cursed as Nate waited for the explosion to settle.

Nate charged again, this time with Barrett at his side. They reached the outer ring of the camp, exchanging fire with two bandits behind a shack. Barrett took a hit to the shoulder, but kept moving, gritting his teeth as he returned fire. When one outlaw fell, his companion bolted.

Inside the outlaw camp, chaos reigned. Pike's men were disorganized, panicked. Supplies burned, horses fled, and the canyon filled with smoke as Royce and two deputies breached the barricade, fighting in close quarters.

Fists flew, and knives flashed, but Nate had eyes only for Pike.

There you are!

Nate broke into a run, dodging rocks and gunfire. Pike turned, saw him coming, and raised his revolver. He fired, and Nate staggered as the bullet slammed into his right knee.

Nate barely slowed, adrenaline overwhelming the pain he knew he'd feel later.

"It's over, Pike!" he roared.

Pike's squinty black eyes met Nate's, and a crooked grin spread across his face—the taunting smirk that had haunted Nate's nightmares. The gang leader bolted toward the canyon wall and ducked behind a boulder.

Nate followed, bullets sparking off stone as he closed in on his prey. His heart pounded as he dodged behind a rock, then sprang out and fired with deadly aim.

Pike spun as the shot hit his shoulder, blood spurting, and his revolver fell to the ground in a puff of dirt.

Nate ran forward, closing the distance, his eyes boring into Pike.

"Ready to face justice?" he growled.

Pike clutched his bleeding shoulder and looked up with a strange grin. His eyes glistened with defiance. "We'll see about that, Sheriff."

Chapter One

Niobrara, Nebraska, Autumn 1887

Seventeen years later

The sun dipped behind the cottonwoods, casting long shadows across the pasture. Nate Holt sat tall in the saddle, boots loose in the stirrups, letting Henry meander along the fence line. The buckskin's ears flicked lazily, tail swishing at flies.

Deck, a half-breed mutt, trotted beside them, nose twitching at every scent that drifted on the breeze. His fur was a patchwork of brown and white, and his short, curly tail wagged up a storm when he was happy.

Everything in its place. No broken gates. No stray cattle. No trouble.

This was the kind of evening Nate had come to treasure: quiet, predictable, with the livestock behaving and no one urging him to round up a posse or make an arrest. His leg twinged at the thought, phantom pain from the bullet Pike had put in him all those years ago.

Those days are long gone.

He patted Henry's neck. "That's it, fella. Let's head in."

Deck barked once, and Nate shushed him gently. "Easy, now. We're done for today."

The cabin stood ahead, tucked into a grove of ash trees, a lazy curl of smoke rising from the chimney. He was looking forward to a warm fire, a plate of beans, and the dog-eared adventure novel waiting beside his rocking chair. The kind with pirates and lost cities—nothing that reminded him of the real dangers he'd faced in his time as a lawman.

Then, he heard it.

Thunk.

Wood against wood.

Deck froze. He gave a low, rumbling growl—a warning of possible danger—and barked sharply.

Nate swore under his breath, more annoyed at the idea of trouble than afraid, and reached for the Colt at his hip. The weight was familiar, although he hadn't drawn it in months.

Intruders were rare out here, but he'd encountered a few drifters. Once, he'd startled a claim jumper up in the hills; twice, he'd surprised hungry fools who didn't know better, ransacking his barn.

He nudged Henry into a trot, Colt raised, and hollered, "This is private property! You've got ten seconds to clear out before I make you regret it!"

Deck barked again, louder this time, pacing ahead like he was ready to tear someone's leg off. The dog raced around the cabin, coming to a stiff-legged stop in front of the cabin and snapping.

Nate rounded the cabin, then stopped Henry with a quick jerk of the reins.

A thin boy stood on the porch, probably no older than twelve. From the looks of his clothes—ragged overalls and dusty shirt—it appeared he'd traveled long and hard. He held a rifle in one bony hand, pointed straight at Nate's chest.

"Sheriff Nate Holt?" he asked in a thin, trembling voice. "From Niobrara River?"

"That's me—and I'd be obliged if you lowered that rifle."

Nate studied the boy's strong jawline and deep blue eyes, reminiscent of endless prairie skies, almost like—but no, it couldn't be.

And yet...

It was more than his eyes or that unruly shock of curly coffee-brown hair—his posture was familiar, determined and stiff-necked.

The resemblance was too striking. It couldn't be a coincidence.

Etta's boy?

Nate swallowed against the desert forming in his throat. "Why are you here?"

"I came to talk."

"Talk fast," Nate said, "and lower that rifle."

The boy hesitated, then slowly let the barrel dip. "It ain't loaded, anyway. My name's Jed—Jed Holt."

The name slammed into Nate like a punch to the gut.

"My ma was Etta Holt," the boy continued. "She... passed last month, an' before, she—she tol' me to come here. Ain't got nowhere else to go."

Nate holstered his Colt, hand trembling slightly. "Etta was your ma?"

The boy nodded. "An' she said *you* were my pa."

Now silent, Deck jumped onto the porch and sat beside the boy, tail thumping once. Obviously, the mutt didn't consider Jed a threat.

Nate stared. The resemblance was there—Etta's cheekbones, her stubborn mouth, and those tell-tale eyes—no mistaking it.

He dismounted slowly, thumping to the ground. "She never told me."

Jed shrugged. "She said you were too busy chasing criminals to be a pa."

Unbidden, Nate's thoughts returned to the night Etta left.

"I can't live like this anymore—it's too hard, never knowing if you'll come back alive when you walk out the door!"

He'd wanted to argue, to beg her to stay, but truth was, she hadn't been wrong. Still, in all the years since, he'd never forgotten her or the love they'd shared.

Silence fell, filling the distance between them with years and regrets.

Finally, Nate cleared his throat. "Go on inside. After I see to my horse, we'll eat—you look half starved."

Jed nodded, slinging the rifle over his shoulder and bending to retrieve a threadbare knapsack at his feet. "Reckon I am."

As he led Henry to the barn, Nate's old injury screamed in his right leg. *One shootout too many.* Glancing over his shoulder, he saw the boy's eyes widen as he limped away.

Nate hurried through his chores, thoughts battling in his head. He and Etta had always wanted children, but after several years of no luck, he hadn't had the heart to upset her by bringing it up anymore. Now, his heart throbbed with conflicting emotions: joy that their prayers had finally been answered; regret at the thought of all the years he'd missed; anger at Etta for keeping this miracle from him.

Why didn't she tell me?

As he removed Henry's tack, Nate wondered if Etta had left *because* of the child. His anger drained away, shame taking its place as he realized he couldn't blame her.

Maybe she thought having no pa at all would be better than losing him to murder at the hands of the Coyote Clan.

The thought sank in his gut while he finished up, then sat there like a lump of lead as he trudged across the yard.

Warmth washed over Nate as he stepped into the cabin, the fire in the big wood range crackling. Jed sat at the table, surveying the room—maybe searching for clues about the stranger who was now his father—while Nate lit the lantern on the table and set a pot of beans on the stove.

Deck had curled up beside the boy, settling his head on Jed's boot.

"What's your dog's name?"

"His name's Deck. Seems to like you, don't he?"

Jed's brow furrowed. "That's an awful strange name."

Reaching for two tin plates, Nate chuckled. "Reckon it could seem that way. It's short for 'Decker.' Got him as a pup from a homesteader who couldn't take the harsh winters. The fella had named him, and I figured not to confuse the pup by changing it."

Jeb nodded and reached down to rub Deck's stubby ears.

"How far did you travel?" Nate put a plate and mug in front of the boy. "Last I heard, your ma had settled in South Dakota. Yankton."

"Yep, been on the road a couple weeks. Hitched a ride once or twice with a wagon headed in the right direction, but mostly, I walked."

That's over forty miles!

A peculiar sensation filled Nate's throat—indignation, maybe, flavored with guilt at the idea of his son being forced to make such a long journey.

Nate inhaled, swallowing the surge of foreign emotion, and forced himself to speak casually. "You come all that way alone?"

Jed shrugged again. "Didn't have much choice."

Nate ladled beans onto the plates and passed Jed a slice of bread. He watched the boy take slow bites, chewing each bite with mechanical purpose. He looked rough, like he hadn't slept in days—clothes torn, boots worn through—but Nate also saw steel; the boy wouldn't bend easy.

He's got a lot of Etta in him. Wonder if I'm in there somewhere, too.

The absence of conversation seemed to magnify the *clink* of spoons to the point that Nate flinched when the fire emitted a *pop*.

"Reckon you're pretty worn out," Nate said, suddenly desperate to fill the silence. "I'll fix you a pallet in front of the fireplace for tonight. We can talk tomorrow, figure things out."

Jed shrugged, abandoning his attempt to lift another spoonful to his mouth.

Nate leaned back in his chair, staring at the boy across the table. *Jed Holt—my son, by name and blood. Almost fifty-two years old, and I just found out I'm a pa.*

It might've been funny if Nate hadn't been so uncertain of what tomorrow would bring.

Chapter Two

Holt Ranch

A week later

The boy hadn't said another word about his mother's death.

A week on the ranch, and not a single mention. Not a question, not a tear. Just quiet obedience. Jed didn't speak to Nate unless asked—and even then, it was short answers. *Yes, sir. No, sir. I'll do it.* He mucked stalls, hauled water, stacked firewood, and fed the chickens like he'd been born to it.

But grief clung to him like a shroud. He walked around silently, stubbornly wrapped inside himself, his grief locked tight.

Nate watched him from the porch, a tin mug of coffee cooling in his hand. Jed moved with purpose, frowning, while Deck trotted beside him like a shadow. Nate didn't know how to pry the boy's heartache loose—or if he should even try.

The September sun rose golden and bright, casting long rays across the dry earth. The air smelled of cracked leather, horse sweat, and the faint sweetness of hay. Cicadas buzzed in the cottonwoods, and wind carried the distant creak of the windmill turning slowly above the well.

It would be another fine day, the kind Nate had cherished since he'd hung up his guns for good. The only blot on his mood was Jed.

He sighed and walked toward the barn, then leaned against the corral fence, watching Jed groom the buggy horse, Molly.

The mare leaned into each stroke, obviously enjoying the attention.

"You know," Nate remarked conversationally, "when I was about your age, I ran off for a whole summer. Took odd jobs, slept in barns, got into a few scraps I shouldn't've."

Jed didn't look up, but the brush slowed against Molly's coat.

"Ended up working for a rancher outside Abilene," Nate went on. "Mean ol' son of a gun paid me in beans and bruises, but he taught me how to mend a fence, how to make my own way. I didn't talk much back then either. Just kept my head down, trying to make it on my own."

Jed finally glanced over. "Kinda know how that is."

Nate smiled. "I figured. That's why I'm telling you. I know what it's like to carry your own weight in this world, afraid to depend on anybody else."

Wordlessly, Jed turned back to Molly as she nudged his hand impatiently, and Nate swore the boy almost smiled as he resumed brushing the mare's coat.

"I'm here if you want to talk," Nate continued doggedly, despite his son's reticence, "and I'd like to know more about you, if you ever feel like sharing."

Jed didn't answer, but he didn't walk away either. That was enough for now, though Nate couldn't help a stab of annoyance; for a moment, he thought he might've gotten through to the boy.

Well, I reckon he's done all right without me so far. He'll talk when he's ready.

Sighing, Nate walked back to the porch, stifling his disappointment as he turned his thoughts to his plans for the day. Supplies were low, and the fence on the north pasture needed new wire, so he'd decided to go into town.

He stepped inside to grab his leather duster, but when he came back out, he noticed dust rising over two familiar silhouettes against the morning sun: Travis and June Rivers, Barrett's young'uns.

They rode hard, their horses lathered and breathing heavy. Travis wore his father's old hat, sweat-stained and sun-bleached, brim pulled low. June's blond curls had been tied back with a limp bow of calico.

His gut twisted before they even reached the gate. He couldn't remember the two ever visiting without Barrett.

Something's wrong.

He thumped down the steps as they rode into the yard. "What's happened?"

Travis dismounted, his face drawn tight. June stayed in the saddle, twisting to scan the horizon over her shoulder.

"Pa's dead," Travis said flatly.

Nate stopped in his tracks. "What?"

"Sheriff Crane found him yesterday morning, Sheriff Nate, out by the creek," June added, tears slipping from her brown eyes, so like Barrett's, to dampen her rosy cheeks. "We think..." She gave her brother a desperate glance as her voice faltered.

"He was shot in the head—murdered," Travis blurted, his lips quivering as he gulped. Leather squeaked as he clenched his gloved hands into fists.

Nate's breath caught. Barrett Rivers had been his loyal deputy for nearly a decade. He may have been stubborn as a mule, but he'd been sharp as a tack, and they'd cleaned up more than their share of messes together—cattle rustlers, land disputes, drunken shootouts in the saloon—Barrett had stood beside him through it all. And now, he was gone.

It can't be true. Dead?

"Could it've been an accident?" Nate asked, though the words felt hollow. Barrett had been too cautious, never letting his guard down a second.

Travis shook his head. "It was murder—I know it. A couple weeks ago, he told us he saw outlaws in town, men he recognized from the old days. Thought they might be after him."

June finally dismounted, hitting the ground with a *thud*. Her divided riding skirt billowed around her slim body as she brushed dust from a blue shirtwaist. "Sheriff Crane didn't believe us, though. Said Pa must be getting old, seeing shadows, and that he was probably just shot by a rustler."

"Pa mentioned something about the Coyote Clan—or what's left of 'em." Travis took up the tale. "Soon as he said it, he got a worried look on his face, like he hadn't meant to let it slip. I remember him telling stories about 'coyotes' when we were younger, but I didn't realize... We just thought he was talkin' about animals."

Dumbfounded, Nate rubbed his right leg as memories rushed through his mind. He'd never forgotten their last encounter with the Coyote Clan—not after he took a bullet to the knee in that canyon bringing Owen Pike to justice. "That gang's been scattered for years. The ones that didn't get the noose are rotting in prison."

"Not all of 'em," Travis countered. "Rumor is, their leader escaped. Pa suspected he'd been rebuilding the Coyote Clan on the sly. Or that's what he hinted at."

Nate remembered the last time he'd seen Pike, over seventeen years ago, bloodied and laughing after a failed ambush meant to free him before he was locked up for good. Barrett had cracked two of his ribs that day in a struggle to get him behind bars. Nate had broken his nose. They'd sent him off to the territorial prison with a warning: *don't come back.*

Apparently, Pike hadn't listened.

Nate felt old instincts stirring, an itch between his shoulders that whispered of trouble to come. It had made him an exceptional sheriff, but there were times—like now—when he cursed his fine-tuned sense of right and wrong.

"I haven't heard anything about that, but even if Pike *did* escape, there's nothing I can do. I'm retired. I had reasons for hanging up my guns."

Including Pike and the injury to his knee.

June's eyes widened. "But..."

"I'm sorry," Nate said. "Truly. Your pa and me traveled through a lot of tough times together. Losing him tears my heart out, but I can't go looking for trouble."

Travis narrowed his eyes. "You think we came for sympathy?" He scoffed. "We're here for *justice*. Sheriff Crane won't help, but we thought *you* would. You were his best friend... or so he thought."

"I know you're scared," Nate said patiently, "and you should be—but I'm not opening that door. I'm too old and worn out to go chasing after outlaws. Barrett and I made plenty enemies. Yes, Pike could've killed him, but it could just as easily have been someone else."

And Jed doesn't deserve to be dragged into that mess. That's why Etta left.

Just then, the barn door opened, and Jed walked out, a pitchfork propped on one shoulder. Deck followed at his heels, yipping happily as he spotted June. He ran toward her, waving his stubby tail like a flag, moans of pleasure deep in his throat.

Jed glanced up, curiosity flickering across his browned face.

"Hello," June offered, reaching down to scratch Deck behind the ears. "I didn't know you hired a hand, Nate."

There was no easy way to say it. "This here is Jed, my son. Jed, meet Travis and June Rivers, my deputy's young'uns."

Travis and June started, their silence heavy at the unexpected news, and June's eyes widened as she studied Jed. Maybe looking for a resemblance to Etta, whom they'd known well.

Travis stepped forward. "You need to take this seriously, Nate. If Pike's back, he won't stop with Pa. He'll come after you, too... and your"—he nodded at Jed—"son."

"I *am* taking it seriously." Despite the fire raging inside, the sudden spasm of pain in his knee, Nate kept his answer calm. "That's why I'm staying out of it."

Travis's jaw clenched. "If you're too cowardly to do anything, I'll avenge Pa myself."

Nate didn't flinch, but fear lodged in his chest. "Travis, I don't think you know what you're walking into. Men like Pike show no mercy. You're too young—"

Not waiting for Nate to finish, Travis vaulted into the saddle and kicked his gelding into a gallop without another word. June's look of disappointment squeezed Nate's heart as she wheeled her horse around and followed a moment later.

Nate watched them ride off, dust trailing them like a shroud.

Jed spoke for the first time. "Was their pa your friend?"

Nate nodded. "He was my deputy, a good friend for too many years to count."

Jed looked down at Deck, then back up, squinting. "He helped people?"

"That's what good lawmen do," Nate said. "Sometimes he hurt them, too, but he didn't deserve to die so soon."

After giving Nate a measuring glance, Jed turned and walked back toward the barn. Deck trailed the boy, his stubby tail at half-mast. They acted as disappointed as Barrett's kids.

Nate stood there for a long time, a slight breeze tugging at his duster, the oppressive weight of old choices pressing down on his shoulders. When he'd quit his job as sheriff, Barrett had accepted his decision, but he hadn't liked it.

"*Justice is in your blood, Nate,*" he'd said. "*You'll be haunted by every outlaw you let go free.*"

"You're wrong, Barrett," Nate whispered, staring down at a rooster pecking near his boot. Losing his best friend should've felt like a punch in the gut, a fist of pain squeezing his heart, but all he felt was numb.

He'd buried enough ghosts; he wasn't ready to dig up more. Not with a son to protect.

Chapter Three

Niobrara, Nebraska

Faith Shaw stormed into the sheriff's office, her face flushed. "Sheriff, I need to speak with you."

Sheriff Lawson Talbot, a burly man with graying hair, looked up from his desk with a bland expression. He gave a deep sigh, clearly annoyed by her presence. "What brings you here today, Miz Shaw?"

Too bad how he feels! I want justice for Caleb.

Faith clenched her fists and drew herself to her full height, trying to stifle her frustration. "I just came back from the general store in Minersville, where Caleb was murdered." Tears filled her eyes as she struggled to blink them away. It wouldn't do to sound hysterical.

"Now, Miz Shaw, we been over this. Caleb was just in the wrong place at the wrong time. He was shot accidental-like. I done talked to Sheriff Crane about—"

"Don't it strike you as odd that my husband was the only bystander killed during robbery? No one else even got a scratch. That don't seem strange to you?"

The sheriff leaned back in his chair, folding his arms beneath the silver star drooping from the chest of his tan shirt—a badge that, in Faith's opinion, he didn't deserve to wear.

"Miz Shaw, Faith, my hands are tied. Caleb was a traveling peddler—he knew the risks. You need to accept that your husband is dead and move on."

"How can you say that?" Faith's anger boiled over; she'd run out of patience for his nonsense. She knew some folks disapproved of her sharp tongue, but if it got justice for Caleb, she didn't care what people thought. "I refuse to believe a random bullet killed my husband. Sheriff Crane found it suspicious, too, but as he's retiring, he told me to come to you."

Sighing, Talbot rubbed his temples. "Faith, I understand you're upset, but you need to let this go. Stop fretting about it."

After taking a deep breath, Faith smoothed her linen shirtwaist with trembling hands and tossed her long red braid over her shoulder. "I'm sorry, Sheriff, but I can't let it go. Caleb was murdered because someone wants my ranch."

Another deep sigh filled the room, but Faith ignored the sheriff's discomfort. He'd told her often enough her suspicions were *"unfounded."*

"You ain't got proof somebody's out to take your ranch. Seems to me, though, a woman alone... Might not be a bad idea to sell out."

Of all the brazen...!

Before Faith could answer, the door creaked open, and Gideon Hart stepped inside. The tall man's slick manner made Faith's skin crawl. The wealthiest man in town, he brandished his fortune like a weapon, battering down anyone in his path. Faith had come to despise his squinty eyes and the thin slash of black hair over his smirking lips.

"Well, well, if it ain't Mrs. Shaw," he said with an impertinent wink, his eyes probing her with a hint of indecency. "How pleasant to see you today. I've just ridden past some of your fine pastureland. Looks like your hired hand is getting a mite too old to repair your fencing. You could lose a lot of cattle that way."

Faith glared at him. "That's none of your concern. Donovan has worked for my husband and I faithfully, and his abilities are in no way diminished."

"Please, I meant no disrespect. I saw your horse outside and thought I'd pop in to speak to you."

"What do you want, Mr. Hart?" Faith asked flatly, though she already had an idea.

Hart stepped closer, his eyes gleaming with predatory intent. "I wanted to offer my help. I'll make you a generous offer on your ranch, enough to leave Nebraska and return to... Where did you say you came from? Kansas?"

"I was born and raised in Nebraska, and I'm not selling the ranch." Faith glowered at him, one hand instinctively touching the grip of her pistol at her waist.

"Just trying to help." He held up a hand. "No need to get your dander up."

"I don't need your help—unless you know why Caleb was murdered."

Hart's leer widened, and he winked at the sheriff, like they shared some private joke. "I certainly don't know anything about that. From what I've heard, stray bullet struck him in the chest during a robbery. A tragic accident."

Faith clamped her lips to keep from blurting out words no polite lady should utter. She turned to the sheriff, hoping he'd speak up, but he stayed silent. Looking at his wary expression, she suddenly realized that he *feared* Hart.

Narrowing her eyes at the sheriff, she declared, "No matter what Mr. Hart believes, I *know* Caleb's death was not an accident. If you won't help me, I'll find someone who will."

The sheriff shrugged. "Calm down, Faith. There's no need to make a scene. You should consider Gideon's offer. A woman alone—"

"You're… you're useless!" she fumed before storming out of the office, biting her tongue against worse language.

As she stepped outside, sunlight momentarily blinded her. She took a deep breath, trying to calm her racing heart. She couldn't believe Talbot could be so lackadaisical about Caleb's death, especially with Gideon Hart circling like vulture, waiting to pick her bones.

I can't give up now.

Fresh tears filled her eyes. Some days, it was like Caleb had never died; others, like she'd been alone for years.

It felt like just yesterday when she'd met the dashing, sweet-talking Caleb Shaw. Papa had been dead for four years, and she and Mama had settled in Bellevue. Mama had taught in the one-room school while Faith clerked in the small general store. Caleb had come in to sell pots, pans, and other kitchenware.

After a year of looking forward to his visits, Faith had joyfully accepted his proposal. The only dark spot on her joy had been moving to Niobrara, leaving Mama behind.

Caleb's late pa had left him a fine, but struggling, cattle ranch where they started married life. When Caleb traveled, selling his wares, Faith and their loyal hired man, Donovon Burke, kept the home fires burning. They'd shared big dreams and made joyful plans—until Caleb's recent, untimely death.

I'll never sell, especially not to that awful Gideon Hart!

Faith had to keep Caleb's dream alive, to honor his memory. The ranch was more than just a piece of land; it was Caleb's legacy, a reminder of the hard work and dedication of his father before him. The lush pastureland, old barn, and small herd of cattle were all reminders of the life she and Caleb had built together.

Every morning, as the sun rose, casting a golden glow over the fields, Faith woke with a new sense of purpose. She wouldn't let the ranch fall into the hands of someone like Hart, who saw it merely as a pile of dirt and rock—one more acre to sell to the railroad.

Gideon Hart was a shrewd businessman with a reputation for getting what he wanted. This was only the latest of several offers to buy the ranch, each more tempting than the last. However, she'd seen the railroad transform other towns, bringing a wave of destruction, turning peaceful, tree-lined streets into piles of dirt and rock to lay the silver tracks. Settlers were displaced, forced to move on, their dreams abandoned.

She was determined not to let that happen to her—*their*—home.

She reached into her brown skirt and pulled out a shopping list. She'd come into town to stock up on supplies, but her temper had gotten the better of her, and she'd decided to pay Sheriff Talbot another visit—not that anything had come of it.

I'll visit Lydia at the general store. Maybe she'll have some ideas.

Chapter Four

After Travis and June left, Nate fought back restless frustration and tried to figure out what to do with the day. Eventually, he decided to stick to his plan to ride into town for supplies.

The last week had been filled with ups and downs, not the least of which was Jed's arrival. *I'm too old for this. All I want is peace and quiet. Barrett was one of the best friends I ever had, but I can't afford to tussle with a gang—I've got Jed to think about now. Of course, if it is Pike... I reckon I should make sure he ain't coming for me next.*

Nate headed into the barn and led Henry from his stall. Jeb worked nearby, pitchfork spreading sweet-scented straw into a stall.

"I'm goin' into town for supplies. Want to come along?"

Even before Jed shook his head, Nate had known what his answer would be.

"Reckon not. Thought I might try fishing in that creek, if you don't care."

"That's fine. I shouldn't be long." He'd just slung the saddle over Henry's back when the boy startled him with a question.

"You gonna go after that man—the one who killed your friend? Before he comes after you, too?"

Nate made himself take a deep breath. He forced himself to speak gently, although his voice shook from the strain of holding in his anger.

"No matter what Travis and June think, they don't know who killed their pa, if anyone did. Me and my deputy had lots of enemies in the past, but most of 'em are either dead or in prison." He managed what he hoped was a reassuring smile. "Don't you worry. Nobody wants to go after a used-up old lawman like me."

Jed's blue eyes studied him with familiar intensity, the same way Etta used to scrutinize him. When he spoke, it could have been his mother's scolding voice putting him in place.

"Hope you're right. Done buried Ma. Reckon I don't wanna bury a pa, too."

***

Nate spent the ride into town warring with grief over his friend and guilt about not helping Barrett's kids. *It's not like I know who killed Barrett. It's been months since I've talked to him. If Pike had escaped, surely Sheriff Crane or Talbot would've sent word.*

By the time Nate had dismounted and tied Henry to the hitching post at Lydia Burke's General Store, his mind was a hundred miles away. He'd just taken a step up the wooden steps, shaking trail dust from his leather duster, when a whirlwind rushed out the door and slammed into him.

Grunting, he reached out to steady a slight, wiggling body; a second later, the woman tumbled into his arms, a split sack of cornmeal showering them both. Yellow dust sifted down, and Nate felt grains settle in his beard and eyebrows. Coughing, he tasted the meal as he opened his mouth.

"I'm so sorry," the woman apologized breathlessly, though she sounded more irritated than sincerely regretful.

Already in a foul mood, his head pounding, Nate snapped, "Why don't you look where you're going?" He coughed again, brushing grit from his beard.

"Why don't *you*?" she retorted, green eyes blazing. "If you hadn't been blocking the door, I wouldn't have bumped into you!" Flipping a long auburn braid over her shoulder, she glared and brushed cornmeal from her skirt.

"I was minding my own business when you came barreling into me! How am I supposed to get this off my coat?"

"Just brush it off—it's not whitewash! I don't know why *you're* complaining—now I've got to buy more!" With that, she flounced off, pulled herself onto a paint mare, and rode off.

Nate muttered under his breath. *She's a brazen one.* As he wiped yellow dust from his boots with the back of a pant leg, he couldn't get those green eyes out of his head, the auburn hair framing healthy pink cheeks, firm lips, the dogged tilt of her chin.

Too bad she's so disagreeable. She'd be a beauty if she wasn't all wrinkled in frowns and ill-tempered.

Finally managing to dislodge most of the cornmeal, he headed into the general store. As the bell tinkled his entrance, he greeted Lydia Burke. "Mornin', Miz Burke. I'm in need of a few supplies."

"Morning, Nate." The apple-cheeked woman grinned. "You growing moss out on that ranch of yours yet?"

It was her standard joke, that he'd settled for a quiet life like a rock at the bottom of a stream—good for nothing but growing moss.

"Oh, I'm workin' on it." He decided not to mention Jed just yet. Lydia had a talent for spreading gossip faster than wildfire. "Here's my list." He pulled it from his pocket, along with a sifting of cornmeal.

Lydia raised a brow, but didn't comment. "Let me get that started for you."

A short time later, Nate finished up and loaded the brown-wrapped packages into his saddlebags. The new coil of barbed wire, he draped over the saddle horn.

Next time, I best bring the wagon.

"Sorry, Henry. An old fella like you don't deserve to be treated like a pack mule." He gave the long-suffering horse's coarse black mane a scratch. Henry whickered and tossed his head.

Feeling the need for a friend to talk to, Nate left Henry tied to the hitching post and walked the short distance to the Gold Dust, his friend Royce Tate's saloon.

Royce had been a scout in the War between the States. Afterward, he followed the lure of silver and gold out west, settling in Niobrara about the time Nate was elected sheriff. They'd ridden miles together on different posses. While Royce might seem gruff to some, his heart was as soft as quilt batting. He was one of the few people Nate felt comfortable confiding in—with Barrett dead, maybe the only one. It was a sobering thought.

Despite the heat outside, the saloon felt as cool and dark as a cave. This early in the day, only a couple men sat at one of the wooden tables, finishing up plates of steak and scrambled eggs. Whiskey, tobacco, and damp sawdust pinched Nate's nose as he walked inside, blinking in the dim light. He walked up to the weathered bar and leaned against the edge. The distant clink of glass bottles drifted from a storeroom.

Before long, a short, barrel-shaped man backed through the door wearing a starched bib apron over a faded plaid shirt and well-worn trousers. As usual, his shock of white hair appeared to have survived a tornado, surrounding a ruddy, chipmunk-cheeked grin.

Royce's bushy eyebrows rose over cobalt eyes with a welcoming twinkle. "Nate!" he boomed, setting two bottles of whiskey on the bar. "Haven't seen you in a dog's age! Where you been keeping yourself?"

"Well, mostly working on the ranch."

Royce held up a bottle. "Want a drink?" He winked. "Best stuff money can buy."

Nate nodded.

"Figured I'd see you before now. What's been going on out your way?"

Nate waited until Royce had poured his drink before sharing the terrible news. "I guess you didn't hear. Barrett's dead."

"Dead!" Royce's eyebrows shot up as he frowned. "How did that happen? When?"

"Travis and June rode over this morning. Said Sheriff Crane found him yesterday. They think he was murdered."

"Murdered?" It usually took a lot to shock Royce, but Nate could tell that the news had shaken him to his core. "I can't hardly believe it. Why?"

Nate took a sip of whiskey and felt the warmth burn down his throat. "His young'uns thought he'd seen some outlaws from the old days. Barrett hinted somebody was following him." For courage, Nate belted down another swallow. "There's something else. Travis heard rumors that Owen Pike escaped from prison. You heard anything like that?"

"Not a word. It's been about seventeen years now, right?" Royce seldom drank, but now, he poured two fingers in a glass and tossed it down. "Seems like only yesterday we finally caught him. That was a day I'll never forget."

A spasm of pain gripped Nate's leg, an echo of the bullet he'd taken to the knee; it often felt achy and stiff, especially when the weather turned cold. *Pike left me with a reminder I'll never forget.*

A chair scraped across the wooden floor behind them as a voice called, "Thanks for breakfast, Royce. See you again next time we're through town."

Royce lifted a hand in farewell. "Couple of drummers out of San Antonio," he explained as the men tossed coins on the table and left. "They're usually up on all the news, but they never said a word about Pike. Ain't somethin' I expected to hear today. Or that Barrett…"

Nate decided it was time to share another revelation. "About a week ago, I got some unexpected news myself. Boy showed up on my porch saying Etta died and sent him to me." He finished the whiskey in a choking gulp. "He's my son."

"Your—what?" Again, Royce's bushy eyebrows rose, and he studied Nate's face with a curious squint. "You reckon he's tellin' you true? Etta hightailed it outta here over a decade ago. Plenty of time to find herself another man."

"It's been twelve years, and the boy—Jed—says he's twelve. I'm certain he's mine. Be just like Etta to keep him from me, knowing how much I wanted a son. Might've even been one of the reasons she left. It's just…"

He took a deep breath, trying to come up with words to explain how he felt. "Well, I gotta be honest, Royce, I got no idea how to talk to the boy. He won't hardly speak to me. Not tellin' what Etta told him about me all those years. I'm not sure he'd have come at all if he had anywhere else to go. I'd like to be a pa to him, but I don't know how to reach him."

Thankfully, Royce took time to give the matter some thought. He took a damp rag and wiped down the bar, his brow crinkled. "Seems to me, you need to find something you and the boy can do together. Fishing, maybe target practice? He know how to shoot?"

When Nate shrugged, Royce went on, "Might be a way to get him talkin'. Been a few years, but I still recall goin' hunting with my own da. Best memories of my boyhood. Spend time getting to know him, maybe he'll come around."

"Hmm... Maybe."

At that moment, the batwing doors swung open; Nate turned to look over his shoulder as three strangers walked inside.

"That's an odd-looking bunch," he muttered.

One was tall and lean, with a scar running down his left cheek. His cold eyes scanned the room with predatory calculation. Another, shorter but stockier, sported a thick black beard that barely concealed a lopsided scowl. His hands rested near the grips of twin revolvers, as though hoping for a reason to draw. The third, a wiry, dark-eyed man, looked to be a mix of several races. His fingers drummed incessantly on the hilt of a knife in a leather scabbard slung low on his hips.

Nate took a good look, the lawman still inside him alert. These men were trouble; he could almost smell it. They moved into the empty saloon like wolves on the prowl, looking for trouble.

Deliberately turning his back, Nate clenched his glass and gave Royce a warning look. If the men had robbery on their minds, he and Royce would have to persuade them otherwise.

"What'll it be, gents?" Royce's voice echoed in the empty saloon as he casually lowered his hand. Behind the bar, Nate knew, Royce kept a loaded twelve-gauge shotgun handy.

"Might be you can help us," the lean man with the scar drawled in a Southern accent. Then, he drew his gun, the metallic *click* of the hammer echoing ominously through the room. A cruel smirk twisted his lips as he lifted the gun, aimed at one of the kerosene lamps behind the bar, and mouthed, *Bang!*

The other two chortled.

"I'd advise you not to shoot that in my saloon," Royce said sternly, "unless you want more trouble than you bargained for."

Nate reached for his own gun, his movements deliberate and confident. He turned and leveled his Colt with calm authority. "You best listen." He stared the rough trio down. "Unless you came in for a peaceful drink, I'd suggest you leave now."

Momentarily taken aback by Nate's words and the Colt pointed at them, the strangers exchanged glances. A smirk played on the scarred man's lips as he holstered his gun. "Don't get all riled up, now. Just havin' a little fun, is all."

Royce scowled. "Have your fun somewhere else."

"We'll be going," he answered, "but remember this, Nate Holt: we'll be back—maybe sooner than you think."

As they turned to leave, a ripple of surprise went through Nate's body. *How do they know who I am?* The encounter had shaken him; it hinted at a past Nate had hoped to leave behind.

Is this what happened to Barrett? Maybe I should have taken Travis's warning more seriously.

"What the devil was that all about?" Royce exclaimed once the batwing doors had swung shut.

Nate shook his head. "No idea, but seems like I best be finding out. If the rumors about Pike are true..." He poured another drink and downed it in a burning gulp. "And maybe I need to figure out who was following Barrett. If the Coyote Clan is bent on vengeance, I got a feeling this ain't the last visit I'll be getting."

Chapter Five

Holt Ranch

The following morning, Nate woke with a new sense of determination. His conversation with Royce had left him with a lot to think about. So had the encounter with the strangers.

After leaving the Gold Dust, he'd gone to see Sheriff Talbot. *Not that it did much good.*

"Well, Nate... There ain't a whole lot I can do if the strangers didn't cause any actual harm. They was probably just cow hands showin' off. Mighta been drunk 'fore they even got to Royce's place. I'm not sure what you want me to do."

As the conversation devolved into more of Talbot's platitudes about "good ol' boys," Nate had struggled to rein in his anger; his disgust had grown too big to control. Without even a goodbye, the sheriff's mumbling ringing in his ears, Nate had stormed out the door and rode home.

He'd tossed and turned most of the night, twisting from one useless thought to another, before a rooster's crow jolted him from a fitful doze to the gray tatters of morning.

"Another day," he muttered as he built up a fire in the cookstove. Not much he could do about the strangers or the sheriff's dismissive attitude.

The boy, however...

Nate decided it was time to try with Jed again, hoping to break through the boy's tough exterior. He made a hearty breakfast, hoping the smell of eggs and coffee would lure Jed to the table.

The boy had been up before dawn, milking the cow, Iris, feeding the chickens, and hiding out in the barn. He seemed to spend a lot of time off to himself. Most of the time, Deck followed. This morning, though, the mutt danced around Nate's feet, eagerly awaiting his own meal.

"You know who butters your bread, don't you, Deck?"

The dog wagged his stubby tail, pink tongue lolling from the side of his mouth.

As Nate set the table, Jed appeared, expression as brooding as ever. Like Etta's, the boy's silence was thick enough to cut with a meat cleaver.

But I'll be durned if I won't try to be friends somehow.

"Morning, Jed," he greeted with a smile. "I was thinking we could do some shootin' practice today. Maybe knock down some tin cans after breakfast. What do you say?"

Jed's eyes lit up briefly before he quickly masked his excitement. With a straight face, he nodded. "Sure," he replied, forking up a bite of eggs. "I ain't never done much shooting. Reckon that could be fun."

Nate felt a small spark of hope. He couldn't help but chuckle at the way the boy tried to sound like he didn't care. "Great! Finish your breakfast, and we'll head out."

Jed polished off the food faster than Deck, then helped clear the table.

"We can wash the dishes later," Nate said when the boy poured water into the wash pan. "Let's get out while it's cool."

Nate retrieved an old rifle and a box of ammunition, and they spent the morning setting up targets on a fallen log in the south pasture. Jed had obviously never done much shooting—

if any—but Nate offered patient advice, showing him how to hold and load the gun, as his pa had taught him.

"First thing to learn is, never point a gun at anyone—unless you plan to shoot."

At first, Jed was hesitant, but as the morning went on, he began to relax and even seemed to be enjoying himself. Nate watched him, feeling a sense of mingled pride and relief. Maybe they could make this work after all.

"Keep your elbows steady," he instructed, putting his hands over Jed's on the rifle's grip, "and don't forget to breathe. Just aim and take a clear shot."

Jed listened intently, his concentration evident. After several attempts, he finally managed to hit a small can. A smile broke out on his face—the first genuine smile Nate had ever seen from him.

"I hit it! Didja see that? Near about knocked it off that log!"

Deck pranced around, barking and wagging his tail.

"Nice shot!" Nate praised. "You're getting the hang of it. Maybe we can go hunting later, catch a rabbit for stew. How'd you like that?"

Jed's smile faded, his sunburned nose crinkling up. "Ma didn't never let me hunt like the other fellas at school. Some of 'em called me a sissy. Ma didn't like guns."

Nate sighed. How well he knew Etta's deep aversion to guns.

"You'll get shot one day, and they'll carry your body home in the back of a wagon," she'd wailed one night. *"I can't take it, Nate!"*

"I'm sorry them fellas picked on you. Your ma... well, I reckon she had to patch me up one too many times, so I reckon

41

I can't blame her. What you got to understand is that a gun is a tool, like a hammer. A man can use it for good or evil."

Nate took a deep breath. "I know things have been tough for you, losing your ma and coming here. They've been tough for me, too. But we're in this together, and we need to find a way to make it work."

Jed finally looked up, his eyes filled with a mix of anger and sadness. "You don't understand. You don't know what it's like, growing up without a pa."

Nate felt a pang of guilt. He'd grown up in Missouri, and while his pa had ruled the farm with a strict hand, he'd been fair and kind. Now, here *he* was, so focused on his own struggles that he hadn't even tried to understand what his own son was going through.

"You're right, I don't—but I want to. I want to understand, and I want to help. I figure it's strange being here, since we don't know each other too good. But we will."

Jed's expression softened slightly, but he still looked wary. He reached down for a blade of grass, then put it between his lips and chewed. "Ma used to talk about you bein' sheriff. Did you like it?"

"Oh, I reckon I did. I was good at it."

"You ever shoot anybody?"

Too many.

"When I had to shoot, I did. A sheriff swears to uphold the law. Sometimes that means you need to use a gun."

Before Jed could ask another question, Nate looked up at the sound of riders galloping toward the ranch. The horses came fast, churning up a cloud of dust.

What the devil...?

Deck snarled and growled, showing his teeth.

"Down, Deck!" Nate ordered. "Stay!"

Three men, faces masked with red bandanas, rode into the barnyard. Nate gaped as the men split apart and rampaged around the yard, destroying his property. One yanked down the clothesline where he'd hung a couple clean shirts and trousers. Another galloped through the flock of hens, sending them shrieking and squawking as he sailed an axe into the tar-paper roof of the coop. The rooster gave a holler fit to raise the dead and sailed into a nearby cottonwood. The third rider headed for the rain barrels, shooting holes in the sides. Water gushed out, pooling into a muddy puddle by the porch.

Durn them! I just hauled that water from the well!

The riders didn't speak, just rode around like drunken cowhands intent on mischief, knocking slats from the corral fence, shooting out the cabin's windows, knocking down the woodpile.

"Stay here," Nate ordered Jed, grabbing his gun and running toward the commotion. "Keep hold of Deck—don't let him loose!"

Nate fired a warning shot into the air. "Get outta here, you varmints!" It took him longer than he'd have liked to cross the pasture, skirt the corral, and confront the masked men.

To his surprise, the riders turned and rode off, dragging the clothesline—and his best pair of trousers with it—through the mud. On their way to the road, they deliberately tromped through his garden, squashing tomatoes and onions—just for spite, it appeared—all without a word.

Nate fired again, but the men were nothing but a cloud of dust and distant shapes on the horizon.

Jed came running up, ashen-faced. "Who were they? Why'd they come here and..." He waved a limp hand at the destruction. Beside him, Deck barked and jumped around, stiff-legged, clearly ready to tear the intruders to the bone if Nate gave the word.

"I don't rightly know."

Travis's warning came back to haunt him.

Am I next? I sure won't wait around to find out.

The strangers in the saloon came to mind, too. They'd spoken his name and promised trouble. Maybe the sensible thing would be to find out who they were and what they had stuck in their craw.

"Jed, take Deck and go down in the root cellar. If those men come back, don't come out."

"What are you doing?"

"I'm going to follow them. They came here for a reason, and I plan to find out what it is." It didn't take long to throw a saddle blanket and saddle on Henry's back. After watching to be certain Jed obeyed, he headed in the direction the riders had gone.

The day he'd hung up his badge for good, Nate bought a quiet ranch about ten miles out of town. He knew there were neighbors nearby; sometimes, coming home from town, he caught a whiff of their cookfires or noticed cattle in the pastures. But he hadn't made anyone's acquaintance—there was no need—so he had no idea who lived down the rutted road he traveled.

I wanted peace and quiet, to be left alone. Not chattering visitors.

It was easy enough to track the men; they hadn't even tried to cover their trail. It had been a dry summer, and clear hoofprints marked the way, almost like painted signposts. The trail ended at a tidy ranch tucked between wind-worn hills: a trim log house, cedar-shingled barn, and a corral that smelled of manure and the sweet, musty odor of sunbaked straw.

As it turned out, Nate didn't need to hunt for the masked men. As he reined Henry to a stop, his eyes widened at the scene before him. The three riders who'd just attacked his ranch hadn't bothered to hide or try to escape.

What in tarnation...?

One man sat rigidly atop a black Quarter horse, knuckles taut around the reins. He held two other horses while his companions wrestled on the ground, hammering their fists into an older man sprawled in the dirt. Their masks hung limp around their necks, forgotten, revealing faces contorted with rage as their fists hit bones. Blood speckled the dust like raindrops.

Fury surged through Nate's limbs; his chest tightened, and his jaw locked. Righteous anger flamed his face as his breath came fast.

Where have I seen them before?

He raised his revolver and fired into the sky, shattering the tableau like a cannon. Horses shrieked and danced sideways.

The attackers froze mid-blow, their eyes snapping toward the sound. Then, they scrambled into their saddles, flinging curses back like stones as they tore across the field. As they thundered past, Nate got enough of a look to identify them as the strangers he'd seen in Royce's saloon.

Nate swung down from Henry and ran to the man slumped against the corral fence. Dirt streaked his face. One eye was swollen shut, the other glassy with pain. Blood oozed from his puffy lips and a wound across his forehead.

"You all right?" Nate asked, crouching to steady the man with both hands, wiping away blood to get a good look at his features. There was something familiar about the stocky body and bushy mane of dark brown hair around a weathered face.

Groaning, the man nodded, then winced. "Thanks to you—sure glad you rode along when you did."

I know that voice.

"Mr. Burke?" Nate remembered Royce mentioning that the storekeeper's husband helped a widow as a hired hand. "No need for thanks. Just glad I got here in time. I didn't realize you worked so close to my place. Whose ranch is this?"

Donovan Burke spit out a mouthful of blood, along with a tooth. "It belongs to Miz Shaw. Son, can you give me a hand? My knees are about to buckle."

Nate eased an arm around Donovan's back and helped ease him to the ground. "Easy now. You're bleeding like a stuck hog."

The older man flinched, dabbing at his mouth with a trembling hand.

"What was that all about?" Nate asked, scanning the road where the riders had vanished. "Who were those men?"

"Trouble." Donovon spit out another mouthful of blood. "More trouble than Niobrara's seen in a long time."

Chapter Six

Shaw Ranch

A short time earlier

The sun rose, hot and blistering, beating down on the dry earth as if determined to suck out every drop of moisture. Faith wiped sweat from her brow with the back of her wrist, her hands dusty from digging up potatoes. She'd started in the cool, fresh dawn to pick the garden vegetables ready to store, but other chores had distracted her along the way.

Her braid hung, limp and itchy, along her neck. She'd shoved her damp calico sleeves up past her elbows. If the hired hands hadn't been around, she might've been tempted to take off her long dress, strip to her shimmies, and dunk herself in the cool waters of the stock tank.

Might just do it anyway.

"Soon as I carry these potatoes to the house, I'm gonna wash 'em off." She made a little song out of it, something Mama had taught her to make chores go faster. "Wash 'em off and cook 'em for supper. Ham and taters for supper."

She was halfway to the well when shouts startled her from the pleasant mood.

It wasn't the usual kind of yelling, like the younger hired hands roughhousing near the creek or hollering when an animal escaped from the corral. These shouts were sharp, panicked.

Then, her ears caught the thuds of fists hitting flesh. Cries of pain.

A second later, a loud retort shattered the afternoon. Before she could catch her breath, the sound of pounding hooves approached, harness jangling, curses flung into the wind. She choked as three men galloped past, leaving an ominous cloud of dust in their wake.

For a heartbeat, Faith stood rooted to the spot, breath frozen in her chest. Fear surged in her throat, joining the grit smothering her windpipe. The bucket slipped from her fingers and clattered against the hard-baked ground, scattering potatoes in a wild jumble.

Shaking herself, she ran forward, boots skidding, one heel catching on a tater. She stumbled, grabbed up her long skirt, then resumed her charge.

Dust swirled around her legs as she hurried past the corral, the sharp tang of manure and sunbaked wood filling her nose. Her heart slammed against her ribs with every step, a frantic jab of dread at what she'd find. She rounded the barn and stopped in stunned disbelief.

Donovan Burke, her faithful hired hand, slumped against the fence, blood dripping down his cheeks. Kneeling beside him was the man she'd bumped into at the general store last week—the one with eyes like still lake waters and a trim beard: Nate Holt, the ex-sheriff. After her embarrassing blunder with the cornmeal, she'd asked Donovan his name.

What is he doing here? Did he beat Donovan? No, it must've been those riders.

The ex-sheriff looked up as she approached, and for a moment, her breath fluttered in her throat. Heat flooded her cheeks as she remembered their last meeting. His gaze was sharp, considering, but not angry as when he'd been dusted in cornmeal. His shirt was bloodied, his hands stained red, but he moved with gentle purpose, tending Donovon's wounds—like he'd done this countless times before.

"You hurt, ma'am?" he asked as he pressed a strip of cloth to Donovan's temple. It took Faith a bewildered moment to realize he'd ripped the cloth from his shirt.

"What? No—I was in the garden. Donovan, who did this?" She dropped to her knees beside him, ignoring the sting in her palms as they hit the rocky ground.

Donovan reached a hand to his bloody forehead, grimacing. "Pierce brothers—Sterling and Everett, they said their names were—like they wanted me to know and remember. I'd just got the bull back into the fence when they came riding up. Before I could say howdy, the two of 'em were on top of me. The other one just sat there, staring, while they beat me up.

"Why would they attack you, just to leave a message?"

Donovan shook his head, his tongue easing over his split lip. "Guess they wanted to give me an idea what might happen if we didn't listen." He lifted a bruised hand to his swollen eye. "The one with the scar said we better leave the ranch if we know what's good for us, that someone named 'Owen' would make sure we all die like Caleb did if we stayed."

Her late husband's name hit Faith like a slap. Everyone had said it was a tragic accident—just a stray bullet—but now... Was this proof, finally, that Caleb had been deliberately shot?

Swallowing, she finally processed the rest of what he'd said. "Owen...? I've never heard—"

Nate's jaw clenched tight after a sudden intake of breath.

He recognizes that name.

"You know this man?" she asked. "This Owen?"

"I did. Long time ago." His expression had changed. Gone was the calm, confident manner; his eyes were dark, furious, like a lake before a storm, filled with frightening depths. "I thought we buried Owen Pike in prison," he said quietly. "Guess he crawled back out."

"Who is he? Why would he come here?"

Instead of answering, Nate handed Donovon the makeshift bandage. "The sheriff will want to hear about this." A quirk of a grin lifted his lips beneath the cinnamon-colored beard. A flicker of amusement sparkled in his eyes. "Well, maybe he won't *want* to hear, but he will."

For a brief second, Faith's heart lifted. Apparently, Nate Holt didn't like Sheriff Talbot any more than she did.

He stood, brushing dirt from his knees, and for a moment, Faith couldn't look away. He was taller than she remembered, broad-shouldered, with a quiet strength that made her feel both safe and unsettled. The empty spaces in her heart filled with a yearning that caught her off guard.

And why should I think of another man like that, with Caleb only gone a few years?

"I'll ride into town," Nate continued. "Tell the sheriff to round up a posse—if he'll listen. Those men need to be stopped, and we'd best find out what Pike's up to." He looked off toward where the men had gone. "I don't think they'll come back tonight. You should be safe."

Faith nodded, still kneeling beside Donovan. "Thank you. If they do return, we're armed."

Nate paused, looking down at her. "I'll drop in later to make sure you're all right. You want me to stop by the store and tell Lydia what happened, Donovan?"

"No!" Donovan started to rise, but apparently thought better of it and sagged against the fence. "Naw, she'd just worry herself sick. I'll pull myself together, clean up, and ride in later. Just let me sit here a spell while I catch my breath. Those fellers took more outta me than I expected."

"I can take you in the wagon," Faith told him. "It'll be more comfortable than trying to ride. Thank you, again, Mr. Holt, for your help."

After a curt nod, he was gone, his horse whinnying as he rode away from her ranch.

Faith turned back to Donovan, her hands trembling. She tore strips from her apron, pressing them to his wounds, whispering reassurances she wasn't sure she believed. When she dared leave him alone for a few minutes, she hurried to the well and brought back a pail of clean water.

"They said Caleb's name," she murmured as she wiped the blood from a cut on his forehead. "Do you think they..." Her voice faltered, the thought almost too frightening to finish. "Could they be the men who murdered him?"

Donovan's eyes fluttered open. "I'm not sure. I think, more than anything, they wanted to scare us."

"Well, it worked," she said tightly, "but I'm not leaving."

She moved quickly, hands now steady, but breath still uneven. Her fingers knew what to do. Ranch life had taught her how to doctor injuries, but her mind kept circling back to Caleb. To the way his name had been spoken like a warning. A threat of what would happen to her if she didn't listen.

What possible reason could they have to want me to leave? Is that why Caleb died?

She sat back on her heels, watching Donovan's chest rise and fall, slow, uneven, but thankfully alive. His eyes closed, and she left him sitting against the fence. *I'll let him rest for now.*

The barn rose beside her, begrudging a meager patch of shade. The afternoon filled with normal sounds: the rustle of cattle, the distant creak of the windmill, the soft hiss of a barn cat. Farther away, a saucy bluejay shrieked a warning as it sailed into the cerulean sky.

Faith leaned against the wall of the barn Caleb's father had built years ago. She and Caleb had come here to live after they'd married, determined to make Papa Shaw's ranch prosper. They'd spent countless days improving the land and building up the herd.

Faith refused to let their dreams die. She'd refused every one of Gideon Hart's attempts to buy her land. But now...

Arms wrapped around herself; she tried to still the tremors of fear. A cloud passed over the sky, and for one dark second, blotted out the relentless sun.

Oh, Caleb! I don't understand what's happening.

Just then, her thoughts were too scrambled to figure it all out. Caleb was dead. The strangers had said that, if she didn't leave, she would die too. A man named Owen Pike wanted her land—just like Gideon Hart.

The biggest question was one Faith couldn't answer—not yet, anyway.

Why?

Chapter Seven

The sheriff's office hadn't changed much since Nate had last visited: same creaky wooden chairs, same dust coating the windowsill like it had nowhere else to go. It grieved him to see cobwebs dancing in the corners of the ceiling and clods of dried mud on the floors.

As sheriff, Nate had taken pride in keeping his office clean and tidy. If he wasn't mistaken, the straw broom rested in the same corner where he'd left it, years ago. Didn't look much like Talbot put much stock in the precept *Cleanliness is next to Godliness*.

Sheriff Talbot leaned back in his seat, boots crossed on the desk, hat tipped low. He looked like he didn't plan to move anytime soon, no matter what trouble happened in town.

No use beating around the bush.

"I want the truth," Nate demanded as his boots thundered across the dirty floorboards to stand in front of the same desk he'd used, waiting for the sheriff to lift one eye open. "Is Owen Pike out of prison?"

"Yep," Talbot said flatly, then yawned and sat up a little straighter. "Got a wire couple'a days ago. He escaped about two months back. Word is, he's trying to re-form the Coyote Clan."

Nate felt the words settle in his chest like bullets. "Anyone seen him around?"

"Not so's I've heard."

"Why didn't you tell me?" Nate held in the belligerence raging in his chest. No sense ruffling Talbot until he got some answers.

He wouldn't care about my place getting ransacked anyway.

Talbot's eyes narrowed mulishly. "Because I knew you'd come walking in here, lookin' to stir up trouble."

"I'm not looking for trouble."

"Maybe not," Talbot said, "but what if trouble's looking for you? You've got a good life now, Nate. Quiet. Peaceful. Don't throw it away chasin' the past. If Pike comes around, leave him to me."

"He might already *be* around." It took every ounce of Nate's strength not to lean over the desk and yank Talbot across it. "I just came from Faith Shaw's ranch. Three men attacked Donovan this afternoon—beat him black and blue. If I hadn't come along, they might've killed him."

The sheriff's boots thumped to the floor. His rheumy eyes blinked slowly, as if not comprehending the information. His mouth opened, then closed again, the words dying before they passed his lips. For a moment, he looked less like a lawman and more like a coward who'd realized he might be forced to take a stand. "But he's gonna be all right?"

"He will be," Nate snapped, "but the men who attacked him said they had a message from Pike."

"What did they say?" Talbot asked reluctantly, like he didn't actually want to know, but was duty-bound to ask.

"They told Donovon that if Miz Shaw didn't abandon her ranch, she'd end up dead like her husband."

"That don't make no sense. Sheriff Crane said Caleb got shot by chance when the store got robbed. How would that have anything to do with Pike or the Shaw Ranch?"

Nate ground his teeth, fighting the urge to knock sense into the man. Instead, he swallowed hard, clenched his hands at his sides, and spoke brusquely. "All I know is what those men told Donovan. They were there to give him a message from Pike."

"You get any names?"

"Pierce, I think he said, brothers—Sterling and Everett." Nate had thought hard on the ride into town, but he couldn't recall running into the pair before encountering them in the saloon. He couldn't tell by Talbot's expression whether the sheriff had. In any case, the lawman obviously didn't plan to take any action, so Nate didn't see any use in telling him about the attack on his ranch.

"Well, now—" Talbot began, but Nate's patience with the man's nonsense had run out.

"Just thought you should know. Thanks for nothing." Nate spun on his heel and stepped back out into the sun, Talbot's rumblings following him through the door. The last thing he heard as he loosened Henry's reins was Talbot's warning: "Better leave things alone, Nate."

Not happening.

Apparently, if Nate wanted anything done, he'd have to do it himself.

***

The ride to Miner's Glen was long and dry, a stretch that gave a man too much time to think. Henry moved at a steady pace, kicking up a hazy cloud of dust.

Nate sighed, shoving his wide-brimmed hat away from his sweat-soaked forehead. *Sure would be nice to get some rain.*

As he rode along, Nate thought about Barrett. A few years before they'd joined forces, Barrett, his wife, and their young'uns had settled a small homestead in nearby Miner's

Glen. At one time, there'd been a prosperous silver mine nearby, but it had petered out long ago. Still, it was a peaceful village, safe for bringing up children. They'd had a pleasant life until Barrett's wife had died of snake bite the year June turned twelve. Nate had tried to get Barrett to move closer to Niobrara, but he'd refused.

"*Naw,*" he'd say whenever the subject came up. "*Travis is old enough to keep an eye on June, so I'd just as soon stay put.*"

We used to ride this trail together when we were younger, and the world felt like each day was filled with promise.

Memories of Barrett filled Nate's mind as he rode along. He'd had a laugh that could shake the leaves off the trees and a way of seeing the best in people that had made Nate feel somehow lacking.

I should have visited him more often. Now, he's gone, and Pike might be back.

Nate had expected to find Travis and June at their homestead. Instead, he came across them right inside the edge of town. June sat in their wagon near Kline's Feed Store.

As Nate came abreast of the wagon, Travis emerged from the store with a fifty-pound sack of grain over his shoulder. If a look could kill, Travis's glare would've laid Nate in a pine box.

"Sheriff Nate?" June spoke first, surprise in her voice. "What are you doing here?"

As Travis hefted the sack into the back of the wagon, a suspicious scowl appeared on his face. Brown eyes wary, he waited for Nate's answer, arms crossed over his chest like a pouting baby.

"I need to find out what you know about your pa's death."

"Why?" Travis asked, brushing dust off his hands. "You made it clear you didn't want to help us the other day."

Nate excused the boy's rudeness. No sense riling him up before he got the information he needed. "I reckon you need to know about a couple things that happened. I gotta know if it's connected, and... maybe I figured you might've been right about me being next."

A frightened gasp escaped June's lips. Beneath a faded pink sunbonnet, her sunburnt cheeks paled, her lips pinched tight. She gave Travis a beseeching glance with moist eyes. When Travis continued to stand, arms crossed, refusing to speak, June whispered, "We should tell him what we know. Please... He loved Pa, too."

Travis gave his sister a loving look, reached over to pat her hand, and lowered his voice, glancing around as if he didn't want to be overheard. "Follow us down the road a spell," he said. "There's a rundown store where we can talk privately."

After climbing up into the wagon, Travis shook the harness, urging their mottled gray horse to trot down the road. Nate followed until he saw an abandoned building in a shady grove of cottonwoods. Once out of the saddle, he tied Henry to a branch, took out his canteen, and swallowed lukewarm water. It quenched his bone-dry throat some.

He followed Barrett's kids inside, rotting floorboards squeaking beneath his boots. Dust motes danced in the thin slivers of sunshine poking through the broken windows. Overhead, a dove called plaintively from the rafters before sailing out a hole near the chimney with a flutter of wings.

Travis leaned his back against a splintered counter while June stood nearby, letting the sunbonnet fall down her back, biting her lip as she looked from Nate to her brother.

"What do you want to know?" Travis's tone made it clear that the boy had a lot of Barrett in him—headstrong and grit-teeth determined.

He won't make this easy.

"Whatever you can tell me. Who did your pa see, or think he saw? What did he say in the days before his death? Anything that might point to whoever had a hand in his murder."

June spoke first, although she kept glancing at Travis. "I'm not sure we can tell you a whole lot. Pa got it into his head a few months ago that folks were being cheated by the railroad. He heard something in town…" She looked to her brother. "You remember."

With a curt nod, Travis clipped out a few words. "Said something didn't sit right—crooked deals and people getting cheated."

"What kind of deals?" Nate asked.

"Land being bought up too fast for expansion," June answered, twisting her hands in the skirt of her gingham dress. "Pa thought folks were being forced to sell against their will. He didn't say much, just enough to make us worry. A few times, he mentioned the Coyote Clan—didn't he, Travis? But when we asked questions, he acted like we better not know."

Travis cut in. "I've been asking around. Whoever's behind this is hitting ranches, threatening landowners. Anyone who might stand in the way. I don't know anything for certain yet, but Owen Pike's name comes up a lot. There were rumors he escaped, but I don't know if it's true."

Nate wished he could lie. "It's true. He escaped a couple months ago."

"Reckon he's responsible for Pa's death? Or the threats?" June's obvious fear made Nate wish he could wrap her in cotton batting to protect her.

"It's possible." Nate took a deep breath. Even knowing there was nothing they could do, Nate wanted to put June and Travis on their guard, just in case Pike came after them, too. "Some men attacked my place yesterday, but they didn't try to hurt me. Did some damage, tore up—"

"Your son—Jed wasn't hurt, was he?" June clasped his arm in a tight grip, scanning his face.

"No, he's fine. I left him in town today with Royce Tate—you remember, the old scout who rode with me and your pa?"

June nodded, a relieved sigh escaping her lips. "I'm glad he's not hurt. Maybe those men just wanted to frighten you. But I don't understand why they'd damage your ranch. I don't understand any of this."

"That's not all. A woman named Faith Shaw has a ranch near mine, and her hired hand—Lydia Burke's husband, Donovan—was attacked.. I trailed the men from my ranch to hers, just in time to stop 'em from beating him to a pulp."

June gasped and tightened her grasp, but he pressed on.

"They left a message for Miz Shaw—from Owen Pike. They want her off her land."

Travis stepped forward. "It all must be connected somehow, Sheriff. Your ranch, this Shaw woman, my pa's death. If Pike is behind it, we need to stop him before someone else dies. Maybe he's working for the railroad."

"Could be," Nate said, "but you need to let me handle it. Just be on guard, and keep June safe."

Travis laughed bitterly. "You expect me to just stand back after what happened to Pa?"

"You'll get yourself killed if you go after Pike. You're too young and inexperienced to deal with an outlaw like him."

"I'd rather die fighting than live scared the rest of my life!"

Nate knew the remark was directed at him, his refusal to help, but he feared the passion in Travis's eyes. He knew that burning fire to right wrongs all too well; he'd felt it once, too.

But fire didn't always burn the right things. Sometimes it destroyed everything, the good with the bad—and, sometimes, it got a righteous man killed before he could get the justice he craved.

Chapter Eight

Niobrara

One day later

The refreshing wind nipped Faith's cheeks as she rode toward town at daybreak. A brief shower during the night had settled the dust on the road and cooled things off after weeks of drought. Dawn splashed along the horizon, painting the gray-blue sky with breathtaking rays of pale pink and autumn orange.

Faith's mare, Delilah, trotted along with a steady *clip-clop* rhythm. Faith wished her thoughts were as tidy as Delilah's steps, instead of a scattered whirlwind of questions and faces.

Like Nate Holt's.

She hadn't meant to think about the tall, blue-eyed ex-sheriff with the firm jaw and quiet strength. Alas, the peaceful morning, broken only by the soft stirrings of birds, left room for thoughts to creep in.

If Nate hadn't come by yesterday...

Would the men have killed Donovan, then come after her? The idea frightened her more than she'd dared to admit to her hired hand.

True to his words, Nate had returned last night to check on her. For some reason, that simple act of kindness had set her breath racing—especially when he'd handed her a paper sack of cornmeal with a wry tilt of his lips. His teasing voice had gone straight to her heart

"Reckon I owe you this from the other day."

When their fingers brushed as he handed her the sack, Faith's heart had made a funny leapfrog jump, something she hadn't felt since Caleb was alive. Hating the way her cheeks flamed like a silly schoolgirl, she'd tripped over her reply. "Th-thank you."

It had taken all her willpower to pull herself up and answer his questions like an intelligent woman. Yes, she'd taken Donovan home. Yes, Lydia was upset, but Doctor Rhodes had looked Donovan over. He'd heal fine. No, she didn't need him to sleep in the barn.

"We hired a couple boys to help with the cattle," she'd told him. "They sleep in the bunkhouse, so I won't be alone. In any case, I know how to shoot."

He'd glanced around the ranch, nodded, and mounted a golden gelding with a black mane and tail. "I best get on home. I plan to talk to Sheriff Talbot again tomorrow. There's got to be a reason for these attacks. If Pike is in Niobrara, somebody's gotta make sure he goes back to prison."

Before her mouth could form another word, he'd tipped a worn black hat and ridden southward. Faith had hugged the sack of cornmeal to her chest, sorry to see him go, wishing she'd offered him a piece of peach pie.

A deep sense of isolation had filled her, one she hadn't felt in what seemed like an age. Donovan had told her that Nate's wife had left years ago, but for all Faith knew, he was still married.

And here I am, all moony-eyed over a sack of cornmeal. What would Mama think?

But that had been yesterday. In the fresh, dew-spangled dawn, Faith had managed to get a grasp on her emotions. Reins clasped in one gloved hand, she rested the other on the holster around her waist.

I'm a grown woman, not some dewy-eyed schoolgirl! I need to stop dreaming and find answers.

The day before, Faith had asked Donovan about Owen Pike.

"Well, it was a long time ago. Nate Holt was sheriff then, Barrett Rivers his deputy. County had a heap of trouble that year—thieving an' shootings all over. Seemed like the sheriff was headin' out on a posse near every week. When he and Rivers finally cornered Pike, Nate got shot in the leg. He's still got a limp."

"Didn't Pike go to prison?"

Donovan had grimaced as the wagon hit a rut and jolted him with a painful reminder. "Well, now... That there's another story. Pike headed up a gang, the Coyote Clan. Varmints was responsible for a mess of killings from here to Texas."

"Why weren't they all hanged?"

"Most were, after Pike told a judge where to find 'em—saved his own neck by turning in most of his gang. Far as we knew, Pike was gonna die in prison. If he's escaped and rounding up a new gang, we got trouble—like them fellers that beat me up."

That trouble was the reason for Faith's ride into town this morning. Despite Nate's willingness to talk to Sheriff Talbot, Faith had questions of her own, concerning Caleb's death and the threat to her ranch.

Niobrara came into view, and Faith eased Delilah down the street. Several men waved greetings as she passed the livery. Ida's Home Cooking Café perfumed the air with freshly baked bread and frying beefsteak. The excited chatter of two pigtailed girls in crisp white pinafores put a smile on Faith's face. Giggling, they hurried past with their little girl secrets. It seemed like a lifetime ago when she'd be so young and carefree.

She tied Delilah outside the Burkes' house, wondering if Lydia planned to open the general store today. The front door was ajar, voices drifting out.

"Lydia? It's Faith. May I come in?"

"Yes, please—we're in the kitchen!"

Inside, Lydia sat stiffly at the kitchen table, her hands wrapped around a violet-sprigged teacup. Faith had expected to find Donovan with his wife, but instead, Royce Tate stood near the stove, arms crossed, murmuring urgently.

"Faith," Lydia whispered. "I didn't think you'd come today, but I'm mighty glad to see you."

Faith crossed the room and knelt beside her friend, taking her hand. "Of course I came. How's Donovan this morning?"

"He's still asleep. Doc thinks he'll heal fine, but he needs to rest for a few days. He probably won't be much help around your ranch."

"Don't you worry about that. Work can wait. But we need to do something about the men who attacked him. Last night, I was thinking Gideon Hart might be behind the attack. I don't know why he'd use Pike's name, but he's tried several times to buy my ranch."

Royce cleared his throat with a curt nod of greeting to Faith. "That's why I came by. Rumors is, Hart means to buy up land for the railroad. Some folks are being forced to sell. I can't tell you what to do, Lydia," he said, "but you best keep Donovan from gettin' mixed up in this business. Now, if you ladies will excuse me, I'd best get back to the saloon."

The screened door snapped shut behind him; Faith waited until his boots thumped down the stairs to ask, "What was that all about?"

"Oh, Faith, I'm sure you remember the Abernathys. They live on the ranch over from yours." After she nodded, a worried pucker formed between Lydia's eyes. "Royce heard they'd been practically ordered to leave their land. Mr. Hart said the deed was faulty somehow…" She fluttered a hand in the air. "I don't really understand all the legal talk, but Donovan got awful upset. Said he was going to get a posse of his own together if the sheriff wouldn't. Doc had to come give him something to quiet him down. It's put me all in a tizzy."

"I'm so sorry, Lydia. I think Mr. Tate is right. Donovan needs time to heal, but I agree that someone needs to take this seriously. I'm going to the sheriff today. Maybe he's heard something."

Lydia's grip tightened. "Be careful. Whether the trouble is coming from Gideon Hart or Pike's gang, it could be dangerous."

It already is, Faith thought, but didn't want to worry Lydia any further.

A slight breeze ruffled the fringe of hair on Faith's forehead as she hurried back down the street. The sheriff's office was just down the road, windows dusty and porch sagging. Each time she came to talk to Sheriff Talbot, the dirty, unkempt place depressed her. It was obvious he didn't take much pride in being sheriff. The thought put knots in her stomach.

Oh, Caleb! I wish you were here to help.

As she approached the open door of the office, raised voices reached her ears; she recognized one as Nate's.

"You think I'm just going to sit here while Pike comes riding back into town and takes up where he left off seventeen years ago?" Nate yelled. "Barrett's dead. Donovan Burke got attacked, and Miz Shaw was threatened. My ranch was attacked the same day!"

Faith paused at the door, heart thudding. *I didn't know that! He never said a word.*

She hadn't expected to find Nate here, but maybe it was a sign. She dreaded talking to Sheriff Talbot about anything. Every time she tried to talk to him seriously, he acted like he didn't care. But yesterday, Nate Holt had cared—and he'd been sheriff once; he'd fought Pike before.

From the way he was shouting, demanding answers to the same questions she wanted to ask, Nate shared her concerns.

Faith took a step back and scurried around the side of the clapboard building. Instead of wasting her time with the sheriff, maybe it would be better to speak to a *real* sheriff. Nate might not wear a badge anymore, but he had more lawman in his big toe than Talbot had in his stumpy body.

The argument went on a while longer while Faith waited. Although she didn't pick up every word, she caught enough to learn no one knew where Owen Pike might be hiding. It took her a startled second to realize the voices had stopped.

The wooden door banged shut, and Nate stormed down the boardwalk, spurs clanging like gunshots against the planks.

"Mr. Holt!" Faith burst from the alley, skirts flying as she chased after him. "Please wait! I need to talk to you!"

He spun around, face flushed, eyes blazing. "Not now, Miz Shaw. I got a lot on my mind."

She darted in front of him as he turned to leave, planting herself squarely in his path. Mud pooled at the edge of the boardwalk from the morning's rain. *I dare him to shove me aside.*

"I came to speak with the sheriff," she said, "but he's useless. My husband was murdered, and I've always known it.

Yesterday, those men told Donovan we'd die like Caleb. If that isn't proof I was right, I don't know what is."

Nate's jaw tightened. "This ain't a game."

Faith squared her shoulders, eyes locked on his, refusing to let him leave without hearing her out. "I know it's not, especially if someone's coming for my ranch."

"I'm sorry about your husband. I truly am. If I learn anything, I'll tell you—but I've got no answers." Looking toward the saloon, he raked fingers through his beard. Up close, Faith noticed that the rich brown was threaded with gray. "Someone killed my deputy, and I aim to find out why. Right now, that's my only concern."

"Let me help."

He barked a bitter laugh. "How in blazes can *you* help?"

"I can share my thoughts, what I know. Lydia and I were just talking about the Abernathys being forced off their land. Gideon Hart has made no pretense he's buying up land for the railroad. He's tried to buy my ranch several times. I always refuse."

Nate wore a patient yet somewhat bemused look, as if unable to understand what anything she'd said had to do with him.

"Don't you see?" Faith tripped over her words, aware of his boots edging away from her. His long, lean body turned to ease past her on the boardwalk. "What if Hart can't get people to sell to him? What if he's working *with* Pike? Maybe your deputy died because he found out somehow."

That stopped him. His gaze drifted past her, toward the edge of town. Lips pursed, he furrowed his brow.

"Pike could be working for Hart," he muttered. "He always did have more pull than a pan of taffy. Barrett might have suspected…"

He stepped past her, then paused. His hand clamped onto her sleeve, firm but not cruel.

"You best go home, Miz Shaw. If I hear anything, I'll send word—but leave this to the men."

Faith's mouth dropped open. *Of all the brazen—!*

Nate chuckled as though guessing her thoughts, then patted her arm and strode off toward the Gold Dust.

Faith clenched her fists, biting back a curse. She kicked the boardwalk hard, her high-button shoe thudding against the rough wood. Pain brought tears to her eyes, but she refused to cry.

The wind picked up, scattering raindrops and rattling a tin sign reading *J. Wright Gunsmith.* Faith turned toward the horizon, where her ranch waited for her return.

With or without Nate Holt's help, she'd find the truth—or die trying.

Just like Caleb…

Chapter Nine

The Gold Dust buzzed louder than usual for morning; Nate shoved the door open, and it hit the wall with a hollow *thud*. Green cotton curtains hung limply around the wide plate-glass window, letting in a weak spill of sunlight that barely cut through the smoke-filled air.

Five men hunched around a scarred wooden table near the back, wreathed with a swirling haze of stale cigar smoke. Cards flicked quickly between practiced, calloused fingers. One man muttered a curse under his breath; another tapped the table with a chipped boot heel. Whiskey bottles littered the table, along with roll-your-own droppings and a lit cigar laying in a chipped saucer.

The room felt close, heavy with the sour scent of men who'd been drinking all night and the spatter around the spittoon. Nate walked across the warped floorboards, drawing a few sidelong glances, but none of the card players spoke to him.

Royce leaned against the bar, polishing a glass that didn't need polishing, his eyes flicking toward the poker game every few seconds.

"How long they been here?" Nate asked, taking off his hat to run a hand through his hair.

"Yesterday, 'bout noon," Royce answered as he put down the linen cloth and reached for two white mugs. "Want some coffee?"

Nate nodded, giving the men a brief grin. Royce had always been a sucker for a card shark on a winning streak. "Couldn't bear to close when Old Man Varner finally had some good hands, eh? You're soft as mush, Royce."

"Where'd you get that three of diamonds, Newt? I swear, if you cheat, I'm gonna tar and feather you!" Varner hollered, thumping a glass on the table.

Royce stopped, coffeepot in one hand, and waited for the excitement to subside. More good-natured joking followed before the men poured another round of drinks and dealt another hand.

With a shake of his head, Royce took a sip of coffee. "I heard what happened to Donovan yesterday. Went to see him this morning—he was hollerin' like a banshee about getting up a posse if Talbot won't. He's worried about Miz Shaw losing her ranch to Pike's gang."

"I've heard all about it." Nate took a generous gulp of coffee. "In fact, I chased the men who attacked him from my ranch. They rode in, whoopin' it up and headed to Shaw's. Truth is, Royce, I don't have a clue why."

Royce set the mug down. "Donovan could be right. I heard Pike escaped a while back."

"I wouldn't put it past him. The men who attacked Donovan said they had a message from Pike." Nate took a deep swallow of coffee. "I tell you, though, Royce... I can't swear to it, but I'd say they were the ones who came in here the other day, tryin' to cause trouble."

"You don't—" Royce had barely gotten the words out when the batwing doors sailed open, hitting the wall with a demanding *thump.*

Conversation died around the poker table as three men stepped into the room. This time, Nate didn't need to turn around; he caught a glimpse of the strangers in the mirror behind the bar. Just like before, they swaggered in, eyes roving over the men at the card table, Nate, Royce. The same predatory looks, the same trio, including the lean man with the scar running down his cheek, who led the way. His spurs jangled across the hardwood floor as he came to stand beside Nate at the bar. Leaning with his back to the bar, he spoke.

"Well now, if it ain't Sheriff Holt," he drawled in a Southern accent. "You still playing lawman, or did Owen Pike give you a bum leg and end your calling?"

Royce stiffened behind the bar, but Nate raised a hand. "Let him talk. Words ain't never hurt nobody."

The scarred man's companions stood nearby, crowding in, but Nate refused to be goaded into a fight.

Sensing the growing tension, the poker players decided to cut their losses, laying down their cards; one by one, they slipped from the saloon. The trio's leader snickered as the swinging doors flapped shut after the last man.

Cards drifted off the table as his mixed-race companion remarked, "Reckon they dropped the dead man's hand, Everett?"

"Could be." The man leaned in, and Nate smelled tobacco on his foul breath. "I'm forgettin' my manners here. I didn't introduce myself proper the last time we came to call. Name's Everett Pierce." He pointed a crooked finger at the short, stocky man, who Nate now realized was much younger than he'd thought, little more than a boy.

"That there's my brother, Sterling, an' the half-breed is Amos Parsons."

"So, we know your names." Nate lifted his mug of lukewarm coffee and forced himself to take a drink and relax his shoulders. "Anything else?"

They'd given him the same names as Donovan, so he knew to be wary. Whatever they wanted, they were up to no good.

"Yeah," Everett said, "I got a message for you, same as that lady rancher: Owen's got plans—big ones—and you're in the way."

Nate met his gaze, refusing to back down. "Then he should've had someone smart deliver the message, instead of sending a bunch of rowdy cowhands to mess up my ranch."

Sterling chuckled, but Everett narrowed his squinty eyes. "You better listen, Holt, or you might be tradin' your ranch for a pine box. Stay out of it. Let the land change hands. Let the railroad come through. Or you'll find yourself buried under it."

"Consider me warned." Nate turned slowly. "You done?"

Everett straightened. "For now."

"Then give Pike a message from me: I sent him to prison once before—he's living on borrowed time if he doesn't give himself up."

This time, all three burst out in deep guffaws, like he'd told the funniest joke they'd ever heard.

"I'll be sure to tell him." Everett turned, deliberately knocking several glasses off the bar to shatter on the floor. They walked out, boots echoing like a warning

After a moment, Royce poured Nate a fresh drink after a wry glance at the broken glass on the floor. "You handled that better'n I expected."

"I'm not the man I used to be," Nate said. In the past, he wouldn't have let them leave without punching manners back into their sneering faces. "Maybe I've learned what's worth fighting for and what's not. What did you think about that little bit of playacting? Makes me wonder what Pike might be up to next. On my way over here, Miz Shaw stopped me. Suggested Pike and Gideon Hart might be working together."

"You reckon she's right?"

"I'm not sure. I'll have to talk to her again. All I know is, I'll clean this town up again if it's the last thing I do. Barrett Rivers was too good a man to be killed by scum like Pike."

Royce lifted one bushy eyebrow, but didn't reply.

The ride home was quiet, but Nate's mind raced with questions he couldn't answer. Were the Pierce brothers and Amos Parsons part of Pike's new Coyote Clan? Most of the original gang had been hanged; Nate himself had sat in on the trials and watched in grim silence as the scaffold was built and nooses circled seven necks. Pike had saved his own by betraying them to the law.

Just what are you up to, Pike?

"It's a confounded riddle," Nate muttered to himself as he topped the last rise leading toward home.

His eyes saw the orange swatch before his mind accepted the truth.

Fire!

Billows of dense black smoke poured out his barn windows. Flames shot skyward. Angry orange-red tongues snapped and sparked, eating through the weathered wood like a cyclone.

Nate kicked Henry into a gallop, heart pounding. One side of the barn was nearly engulfed, flames licking at the wood-shingled roof, glowing sparks flying into the cloudless blue sky like fireflies. Ash rained down, dusting everything in gray, but none of that mattered just then.

"Jed! Deck!"

He jumped from the saddle before Henry even stopped, running toward the blaze. The heat was unbearable, shoving him away with physical force, the roar deafening.

Where's my son?

Chapter Ten

"Jed!" Nate screamed again. "Deck!"

He circled the barn, skidding through bits of charred wood and ash, lungs burning. The wind whipped embers into the cloudless blue sky like tiny roman candles on the Fourth of July. His voice cracked, raw from shouting, but he kept calling, desperate for any sign.

A blur of movement shot from the pasture, and Nate looked up to see Jed, sprinting hard, shirt half untucked. Deck ran behind him, ears pinned, tail whipping like a flag in a storm.

Thank God—they're safe!

"I saw the smoke!" Jed shouted, breathless. "I was out by the creek, fixing the fence. It couldn't have started more than ten minutes ago. We need to get the animals out!"

Nate didn't waste time. "Hurry, but be careful—douse yourself in the water trough first!"

Jed nodded, plunged himself in the water, and came up dripping.

Together, they charged toward the inferno. The barn groaned, timbers splitting with heat. Molly, the buggy horse, screamed inside, hooves pounding against the stalls.

Jed threw open the gate, coughing as smoke billowed out. Nate grabbed a halter and rushed in, eyes stinging. The crazed horse refused the halter, but thankfully, after a smack on the rump, she galloped out, her frightened whinnies fading into the distance.

Inside, the barn was hotter than a forge. Flames ate into the rafters, raining incandescent particles into the shimmering air.

Iris bolted past Nate, wild-eyed, nearly knocking him off his feet. Jed lunged and missed, then whistled sharply. The milk cow skidded, turning, and thundered out to the open field. Her calf howled from inside, afraid to follow his mama.

"Go!" Nate shouted as Jed hesitated. "Drive the rest of the cows out—I'll get the calf."

They worked frantically, every movement rushed. Jed kicked open stalls to free the livestock as Deck barked and herded. Nate knocked down a burning section of wall so another calf could leap to safety. One by one, the trembling cattle fled into the pasture, slick with sooty sweat. Flames crackled overhead, and the roof sagged dangerously.

"Out!" Nat hollered, snatching Jed back just as a beam collapsed. They stumbled outside.

"Deck's still inside!" Jed screamed. "You gotta save him!"

Without thinking, Nate put an arm up to shield his face and ran back inside.

Near the stalls, Deck whimpered, pinned behind a burning beam. Nate dropped to his knees and shoved the timber aside with a grunt. The dog scrambled forward, tail wagging feebly between his legs.

Nate scooped him up and ran.

A beam crashed behind them, sending sparks flying. The acrid stench of burning hair filled Nate's nose as a needle of pain touched his ear, but he didn't stop to brush it away. He burst outside, coughing, eyes streaming, and dropped the dog.

Deck ran to Jed, gave a weak bark, and lay down on the grass, tongue lolling out. Nate turned back. The barn groaned once more and collapsed. A shower of sparks, ash, and wisps of burning hay sailed upward.

Nate's legs quivered, and he dropped to the grass, sending up a brief prayer of thanks for last night's rain. If this had happened yesterday, the brittle, parched grass would've ignited the whole ranch.

He lay there, chest heaving, watching the fire consume everything. Feed for the winter. Tools to run the ranch. Tack. The milk pails. Memories of building the barn with Barrett and a young Travis.

By sundown, there was nothing left of the barn but charred wood, ash, and smoldering bales of hay.

Ash drifted like dull snow across the yard. The cows huddled near the corral fence, eyes wide, flanks heaving. Deck whimpered, tail at half-mast, his fur charred down one leg.

Jed knelt beside him, stroking his head gently. "It's okay, boy," he murmured. "You did good."

"So did you," Nate told Jed. He turned his back on the ruins, grateful the cabin still offered them shelter. "Might as well go inside and fix supper. Nothing else we can do out here."

***

Nate shifted in his rocking chair, the floorboards creaking beneath him. Jed sat across from him, hunched and pale, staring at the empty fireplace with unseeing eyes. Neither of them had eaten more than a few bites of the fried potatoes and cornbread Nate cooked for supper. The silence between them had stretched too long.

The night was cool, but not enough to close the windows. It would help if they didn't have to look outside and see the small patches of flame as the hay smoldered. Even inside, the smell just about choked them with each breath, a painful, nose-burning reminder of the loss.

Nate wondered if this was another 'message' from Pike. If the men had left the Gold Dust and ridden to his ranch to set the fire. Nate's fingers curled around the arms of the chair so tightly, they ached. The thought of what might have happened to his son filled him with so much rage, he wanted to strangle someone. Not a level-headed emotion for a lawman, even one who'd turned in his badge.

"You did real good, helping me save the livestock," Nate rasped. "You doing okay? Reckon it was scary, but we didn't get hurt, and even Deck's all right."

Hearing his name, Deck thumped his tail. He lay quietly against Jed's foot, a linen bandage around his burned leg.

Jed's jaw twitched, and he blinked slowly, but didn't answer.

"I know things've been hard since you come here, Jed, but if you want to talk about anything..."

Jed's shoulders stiffened. His fingers curled in the fur around Deck's ears. "Why do you care?"

Nate blinked, taken aback. "Because I'm your pa."

Jed looked up, and his expression stopped Nate cold. It wasn't anger, or even resentment; this was something worse.

"You didn't care about Ma. Never."

Nate opened his mouth, but Jed pressed on. "You never even cared how she died. Fire, just like today. Lightning hit the barn, an' she let our horse out, but a beam fell on her leg." Tears poured from the boy's face as the words spilled out like a dam had burst inside him.

"I tried to pull her out, but she was already—" A ragged sob shook his body. "She was already b-bu-burned—her skin *peeled off* in my hands!"

Nate's breath caught.

"She couldn't hardly talk, just crying. Then, right before she..." He swiped a sleeve across his nose, smearing snot on his flushed face. "Before she died, she told me my name was Jed *H-Holt!*"

His voice broke on the last word. He stood, pacing the room like he couldn't bear to be still now that he'd started to spill his secrets. "Before, when I'd ask who my pa was, she'd say she couldn't tell me yet. That she left to keep me safe." He kept pacing, twisting his thin fingers together.

"Ma showed me an old box and told me to open it if anything happened to her. So, after she..." He swallowed. "After, I looked inside and found letters she wrote you. She never mailed 'em, but I figured you never cared enough to look for her, so I wouldn't, neither."

It was a childish rant, but Nate understood. He couldn't figure how to reassure the boy, but Jed kept talking like he couldn't bear to keep it in a second longer.

"You think I came here right away?" Jed laughed bitterly. "It took *months*. I was alone, but tried to make it work. Ate up all the food in the house. I patched the roof with nails I found in the ashes from the barn." He glared at Nate, eyes blazing even as defeat slumped his shoulders. "But it got too hard. So I came here—to you—even though you abandoned me and Ma."

"I didn't abandon you," Nate replied quietly. "I didn't even know you existed. Your ma never told me about you, either."

"She told me you cared about justice," Jed said. "That you were a good man, but she had to leave to protect me. Because of your enemies. Because of the danger. I didn't know what she meant."

Nate's mouth went dry. *Oh, Etta.* His heart thudded in his chest as he remembered the threats. The men he'd put away who swore revenge, like Pike.

"She was scared," Nate said, hoping to make the boy understand. "I understand now. She was trying to keep you safe."

Jed's face crumpled. "All my life, I hated you. I thought you left us. I thought you didn't care."

Nate stood from the chair and stepped forward slowly, as though approaching a wounded animal. "I'm so sorry."

Jed didn't move. His arms drooped at his sides, his face streaked with tears he hadn't bothered to wipe away.

Then, Nate did something he hadn't been able to do in all the years of his son growing up.

He reached out and pulled Jed into a hug.

Chapter Eleven

Jed stiffened at first, then collapsed against Nate, sobbing silently into his chest.

They stood like that for a long time. Nate patted the boy's back, feeling his bony shoulders, listening to his childlike sniffles. He wondered how it would've been to dangle a baby Jed on his knee, pretending to give him a pony ride, like his Pa had. To teach a five-year-old Jed to milk a cow or saddle a horse.

All the simple joys, stolen because Nate was a man of justice, and Etta had feared for their son's safety.

When Jed finally pulled back, Nate kept a hand on his shoulder. "I been thinkin'," he said, voice husky with unshed tears. "Would you like to hear about some of the criminals I've caught in my time?"

Jed looked up, swiping a sleeve across his teary face. "I think I'd like that. Ma never would tell me much about you. She just said you were a lawman, and it was a hard life."

"Son, your ma and me had a lot of bad feelings between us when she left. I'm sorry that cheated you out of knowing me, having a pa." Nate leaned forward and gave his son another hug—brief, but solid and real—then pulled back and patted Jed's back twice

They stood together in silence for a few moments. Then, with a trembling smile, Jed sat down cross-legged by the hearth.

Nate pulled up his rocking chair and sat down near him. "You know," he began, brushing soot from his sleeve, noticing for the first time he must have burned his shirt rescuing Deck. "First time I faced the Coyote Clan, I was maybe thirty or so. Thought I was the best lawman this side of the Pecos. Me an'

Barrett were called in on a posse out of Yankton. The gang had robbed the bank and shot one of the clerks."

Jed turned toward him eagerly, elbows on his knees. "Were you scared?"

"Maybe. I'd already been a sheriff for while, but Pike and his men were ruthless." A faint smile tugged at Nate's lips. "Back then, the Coyotes were just a loose group of outlaws—but they were smart, always two steps ahead of us. Took us six months to figure out how to track 'em."

"How'd you do it?" Jeb's eyes lit up as he stared intently into Nate's face and licked his lips. He smoothed a hand over Deck's head, scratching his ears, and the mutt moaned in pleasure.

"Patience," Nate replied, "and luck. We studied their routine, how they worked. Got close enough to recognize their faces a few times. Owen Pike slipped through my fingers more often than not, though."

"He's the leader?"

Nate nodded slowly. "He was back then, until he went to prison. He's older now, maybe meaner. He's had a lot of time to hold a grudge."

"Are you scared?"

"Maybe a bit. I'd be a fool if I thought I could face Pike again without gunfire." Just thinking about that last fight shot pain through his knee, as though his flesh remembered the bullet.

Jed looked down at his scuffed, mud-caked boots. "It kind of scares me to think about him being around somewhere. If maybe he did kill your deputy. Guess I'm not as brave as you."

"Actually, being brave isn't about not being afraid. In fact, bravery can't exist *without* fear. Bravery means you go ahead and act, even if you're shaking in your boots."

After pausing to let that sink in, Nate continued. "I've caught a lot of outlaws in my time," he said, his voice softer now. "Can't honest say I wasn't too scared to spit a lot of the time. Going against men like Pike ain't like a Sunday picnic. A man would be foolhardy not to be cautious."

A breeze swept through the open windows, lifting the scent of charred wood and odors from the barnyard. The sun had nearly disappeared, leaving the sky streaked with ribbons of orange and violet. Outside, the chickens chattered as they roosted for the night, accompanied by a sleepy cow's low murmur.

"Well," Nate pushed himself out of the chair, wincing as his knee tightened with familiar stiffness. "Guess we best figure out where to put those horses for the night. They ought to be safe enough in the pasture. We just need to make sure they got water and tie that corral gate tight."

"I can do that!" Jed jumped up, startling Deck, who'd been snoozing beside his leg. The wiry dog shook his head with a comical expression, almost like *What did I miss?*

Nate laughed, a deep, genuine sound. *I wonder when I ever felt this content. Not for a long time.* "How about we do it together?"

It didn't take long to check on Henry and Molly; both horses formed dark silhouettes in the fading dusk, snipping off grass as they grazed the pasture. The cattle were used to staying out at night, returning to the barn to be milked. They might be confused come morning, but for now, the livestock were safe. One more reason to be grateful. The barn might be gone, but it was just wood and could be rebuilt.

I didn't lose anything that can't be replaced.

They stood together, watching as the last light faded from the sky. A sleepy bird chittered a goodnight as cottonwood leaves rustled. From far away, a lonely wolf howled a plaintive, mournful cry.

"Might as well turn in." Nate clapped Jed on the shoulder. "Let's get some sleep. Tomorrow, we'll figure out the rest. I guess we'll need to rebuild the barn."

Jed nodded, but before they walked away, he turned to Nate.

"Thanks, Pa."

"For what?" Nate asked, his heart about to burst at hearing that word—*Pa. I waited a long time to hear myself called that..*

"For the stories. For the hug. For letting me come here."

Nate smiled. "You're welcome, son." If his heart had felt any fuller, it might've burst for joy.

***

Shaw Ranch

Faith stood at the edge of the storehouse, boots nudging over shattered glass and spilled grain. The morning sun did little to warm the chill crawling up her spine. The place looked like a cyclone had hit it: sacks torn open, shelves chopped into kindling, the lock on the main door twisted and broken like a bent nail, dollars of feed gone.

How will I ever get through the winter now?

She clenched her fists. This hadn't just been a random bunch of rowdy boys causing trouble; it had been a message.

And I think I know who sent it.

As soon as she'd discovered the destruction, Faith had sent Jackson, one of the young hands, to town for help. She was used to handling problems on her own—most of the time. Today, the burden of worry settled on her shoulders like the weight of the world.

What am I going to do?

Faith's head snapped up as a horse rode in fast, kicking up dust. Donovan dismounted before the animal had fully stopped. His face was grim as he studied the wreckage.

"Durn mess," he muttered. "It's even worse than young Jackson said it was."

Only a few days had passed since Donovan's beating, so Faith had been reluctant to bother him.

"I'm sorry I sent for you. I just didn't know what else to do." Her gaze lingered on the broken lock, which had been pried open with precision. "They knew what they were doing. This wasn't random."

Donovan stepped closer, concern mirrored on his bruised face. One eyelid still drooped, turning from purple to a sickly green. "I'd've come anyway—town's buzzing about Royce's saloon gettin' hit last night. Couple of cowhands roughed up, one thrown clear out the window. Folks say it was some men working for Hart."

Faith turned sharply. "Gideon Hart?"

"Yup. And Pike's name came up, too. Folks're saying he's got a new Coyote Clan together, an' they're delivering 'messages'— same as the varmints who came here." He lifted a hand to the scabbed-over cut on his forehead. "Reckon they mean business."

"Of course they do." Faith's jaw tightened as she placed her hands on her hips. "They're trying to bleed me dry. First, they beat you up—and now, this. If I can't feed my stock, I'll *have* to sell. That's what they want. Or Hart, anyway. He's been trying to buy me out since Caleb died. I don't know where Owen Pike fits in, yet, or if he does. My money's on Hart."

"Times are hard." Donovan ran his hand over his jaw, then poked at the scattered chicken feed with a boot tip. Narrowing his eyes, he shook his head. "Could just be some random claim jumper. Did they take any of the feed, or just dump it?"

"As far as I can tell, it's just ruined. The storeroom will have to be repaired. I'll have to buy new feed—if I can even get credit at the feed store. No, this is personal, vengeance against me. Hart wants this land, no matter how ruthless he has to be to get it."

"Miz Shaw!"

Faith and Donovan both turned toward the corral, where the shout had come from.

"What now?" Faith stormed toward the barnyard, Donovan trailing behind. She'd sent Mark and Leon, two of her hands, to check the barn after they'd discovered the storeroom. As she hurried across the hard-packed dirt, a dozen fearful possibilities beat in her brain.

Even before Mark pointed, she saw the empty pen.

Her heart dropped.

"Where's Brutus?"

Chapter Twelve

"Where's Brutus?" she repeated sharply as dread lodged like a knife in her chest.

My prize-winning bull, too?

Mark looked up, misery plain in his pale blue eyes. "I don't rightly know. We thought he was in the north pasture until Leon remembered you been keepin' him penned at night."

Faith's stomach turned. Brutus was her best breeding bull, worth more than half the herd combined. Losing him would be a catastrophe, even worse than the ruined feed.

She spun on her heel, fury rising like wildfire. "This is too much! If Talbot won't do anything, I will! I won't sit here and watch everything Caleb and I worked for be destroyed. I *won't!*"

Donovan stepped in front of her, hands raised. "Faith, think—they're plainly tryin' to rile you up so you'll go off half-cocked, not thinkin' straight. Don't get yourself killed, too."

"I ain't gonna—" Faith began, but a frantic shout from the bunkhouse stopped her short.

Faith took off toward the bunkhouse; when it came into view, she saw Leon bending over Jackson, the boy she'd sent to bring Donovan. Blood pooled beneath Jackson's torso as Leon pressed a towel to his side.

"Dear Lord!" Faith dropped to her knees and lifted the towel as Jackson clenched his teeth at her gentle probing. Through a slash in his plaid shirt, she could see a deep slice in the skin just above his rib cage.

Feeling faint, she handed the towel back to Leon. "Quick thinkin', Leon. Keep that pressure up." She forced herself to take a slow, deep breath as she pressed her hands to her thighs, attempting to still her trembling. "What happened!"

"He was jumped," Leon explained. "Came back from town and went to check the south fence. Two snuffy fellas was watchin' him. When he asked what they were doing, they stabbed him. He was stumblin' toward the bunk when I found him."

Jackson gasped out, "They—masks—don't... why..."

His eyes fluttered, and his mouth went slack. For a heart-stopping moment, Faith feared the worst until she heard his faint, rasping breath.

"Leon, help me get him inside. He's losing too much blood. Donovan—"

"I'll bring the Doc now." Donovan rushed off, already calling for his horse.

With Leon and Mark's help, they got Jackson settled into a bunk. Faith retrieved a basin of cold water and wiped the blood away, then pressed clean towels to the wound, biting her lip as they turned crimson.

Mark hovered over her, twisting a brown slouch hat in calloused hands. "Will he make it, Miz Shaw?"

"I pray so," she answered. "Why don't you and Leon go search for Brutus? Could be he just wandered off in the commotion. I'll stay with Jackson until the doctor comes."

"If you're sure..."

Faith forced a reassuring smile, feeling miles from assured about anything. "Go on. It'll turn out fine."

The hired hands thumped across the floor and clattered off the bunkhouse porch. Not long after, Faith heard their horses head out to the pasture.

Despite what she'd told the young men, worry formed a knot in Faith's stomach. Jackson's wound still bled, and his shallow breaths barely lifted his chest. Usually, his ruddy face glowed with health, but now, he'd gone so white that purplish veins showed beneath his tanned cheeks.

Who would do this?

Beneath her shock and disbelief, though, she knew it had to have been the same men who destroyed her storeroom and stole Brutus—and her gut told her Gideon Hart had something to do with it.

If he thinks he can scare me into selling, he's got another thing coming.

She looked down at Jackson, then out the window toward the hills where Brutus had once grazed.

"Caleb," she whispered, hoping somehow, he could hear, "please help me. Show me what to do."

***

The noon sun blazed down as Nate rode toward Faith's ranch the next morning. Jed was clinging to the saddle behind him, arms circling Nate's waist. Deck pattered along near Henry's hooves. Every few minutes, he'd scent something and chase off, probably in hopes of catching a jack rabbit. A few seconds later, he'd bound across the grass, tongue lolling as his dark eyes scanned the horizon, ever hopeful.

"Has he ever caught a rabbit?" Jed asked.

Nate laughed. "Not that I recall. Mostly just likes to chase 'em."

Nate hadn't told Jed everything. Not yet. He's awoken that morning with worry deep in his gut, the kind of nudge he'd often felt as sheriff, an itchy sense that something just didn't add up.

Why did the barn catch fire?

There'd been no lightning, no lamps or candles lit. Jed had been at the creek—which meant someone else must've set the fire. *Deliberately.*

Once Jed had fallen asleep, Nate had gone out to stalk around the ruins of the barn. Pieces of wood still smoldered, sending out wisps of smoke. He'd walked the edges until he spotted a section of scorched grass. Bending over, he'd torn off a handful of charred grass and lifted it to his nose.

It reeked of kerosene. *I've never stored kerosene in the barn.* He'd found a clue—someone had used kerosene to feed the fire—but it hadn't answered the most important question: *Who?*

Now, as they rode along, Nate debated how much to tell the boy. While he didn't want to scare his son, Jed needed to be on his guard.

"You wonderin' why we're going to Miz Shaw's today?"

"You said you were gonna tell her about your barn so she can watch out."

"That's part of it. Reckon you're sharp enough to know the barn didn't catch fire by itself."

Jed's chin brushed against Nate's back as he nodded.

"Do you think the outlaw done it? The one you told me about—Owen Pike?"

"I'm not sure," Nate said, wishing he knew some facts for certain, "but I ran into Miz Shaw in town the other day. She gave me a lot to think about. I'd like to talk to her and make sure she's all right. There was trouble at her ranch the same day those strangers ransacked our place."

"That's too bad, but you'll figure it out, Pa."

Nate couldn't help but grin.

They'd just crested the ridge above Faith's ranch when Nate spotted movement in the brush below. He pulled Henry to a halt.

"What's wrong?"

"Shh," Nate whispered. "Might be nothing—maybe a deer or one of Faith's hired hands out hunting."

As the shape moved further into the thicket, Deck growled low in his throat, hackles raised along his back.

"Down, Deck," Nate murmured, then turned his neck and told Jed, "Stay here."

Nate dismounted, drew his Colt, and crept down the ridge. The hard-packed trail muffled his steps, giving away no sound. He moved close enough to see a man crouched in the brush. Nate reached out, grabbed the man's collar, and yanked him to his feet.

Sterling Pierce. One of the troublemakers from the saloon.

The stocky boy squirmed, eyes wide with panic. "Hey! Let me go! I was just—"

"Spying, more like," Nate growled. "Figurin' who's barn to burn next?"

Sterling's silence spoke louder than words. A guilty flush crept over his face.

Time we get a few answers.

Nate let out a piercing whistle; moments later, Henry trotted down the ridge, Jed holding on tight. Deck pranced along, eyes wary, his throat rumbling with a low growl.

"That's enough, Deck."

"Who is he?" Jed asked as Henry stopped beside Nate.

Nate held Pierce. Looking around, he spotted a roan gelding tied to a nearby oak. "Mount up, and don't try anything fancy." Nate showed him the Colt and deftly lifted a small firearm from the waistband of Pierce's trousers.

As Pierce obeyed, glowering with a murderous glint in his eyes, Nate turned to Jed. "His name's Sterling Pierce. He and some friends came to Royce's saloon a few days ago. Hinted they were working for Pike. I think it's time he answers a few questions."

Trailing the outlaw, Nate guided him to Faith's ranch. The main house appeared deserted, although a marmalade cat lounging on a railing opened one lazy eye. As they rode toward the barn, Nate noticed a buggy parked by the bunkhouse.

"Looks like Doc Rhodes's rig," he muttered to himself. "Somebody must be injured."

Just then, Faith walked outside, her skirt and pink shirt splotched with blood. A crimson streak smeared one cheek.

Nate froze. *Is she hurt?*

"Mr. Holt," she said as she stepped aside to let the doctor hurry into the bunkhouse, black bag in hand. "You've caught us at a bad time. It's been an awful morning."

He dismounted, keeping a wary eye on Pierce. "What happened? It's not Donovan again, is it? Did those men come back?"

"No, Donovan's fine." She shook her head, looked down at her bloody hands in distaste. "It's one of the hands, Jackson. Far as we can figure, he was stabbed near the south fence. I sent him to town to warn Donovan about—" She noticed Jed sitting on Henry, then Pierce on the roan. "You brought company?"

"The boy's my son, Jed. The other is one of the outlaws that paid you a visit before. Name's Sterling Pierce—said he's working with Pike."

Faith gasped.

Just then, Donovan hurried up. "Who you got there, Nate? He the one who hurt Jackson?"

"I don't know. I found him spying on the ranch as I rode over here." Nate grabbed Pierce's arm and jerked him off the horse. "But I'm halfway certain he gave you that black eye."

"Why, you—!"

With that, Donovan launched himself at the outlaw before Nate could stop him.

Chapter Thirteen

"Settle down, Donovan—just settle down."

It had taken several minutes to drag Donovan away; the man seemed intent on beating Pierce to a pulp. The two had scuffled until Nate, Faith, and Mark finally pulled them apart.

Now, Donovan stood off to the side, breathing hard, fist pounding into his hand. His eyes narrowed in a glare in his puffy, swollen face.

Pierce eyed him, blood trickling down his lip. The whole time, Jed had watched, wide-eyed, from Henry's back, gaping.

Reckon he's getting the education Etta never wanted him to have.

"Jed, why don't you water Henry and the roan while we talk," Nate suggested to distance the boy from the panting men.

"Yes, sir." Jed slid out of the saddle and reached for both pairs of reins.

Nate gave him a reassuring pat on the shoulder as he walked past. He waited to speak until Jed led the horses to a trough near the barn. After a short warning bark, Deck followed.

"Now let's—"

Doc came out of the bunkhouse, tugging on a black coat. He gave Faith an encouraging smile. "Your man will be fine. I stitched him up, but it's a deep cut, so watch out for infection. With a couple days' rest, he should heal with nothing worse than a scar."

"Thank you so much! I'm so relieved." Faith looked like a weight of worry fell from her slim shoulders. "How much do I owe you, Doc?"

The doctor waved a hand dismissively. "All in a day's work. How 'bout one of your peach pies next time you come into town?" With a wave, he climbed into his rig. "Y'all take care."

As he rode away, Donovan turned back to Pierce. "Now, let's get some answers. Did Pike send you? Are you the varmint who damaged the storeroom and stole Miz Shaw's prized bull? Did you stab Jackson?"

"And burn down my barn?" Nate added, startled to hear about the trouble Faith had. "Or was it the rest of the Coyote Clan?" He tightened his grip on Pierce's collar, narrowing his eyes. "Start talking, Pierce. Who put you up to this?"

"No, honest, it weren't me—none of it! Everett and Amos don't let me do much. I usually stand guard. Please, you gotta let me go—they'll kill me."

Scoffing, Donovan shoved Pierce hard on the shoulder. "And we're supposed to believe you?" He stepped forward, his voice calm but firm as he got control of himself. "You'd better start cooperating, Pierce. We know you and your friends have been causing trouble. If you know what's good for you, you'll answer our questions."

Pierce hesitated, then spat on the ground. "It was Pike. After he escaped from prison, he decided to round up a new Coyote Clan. Me, my brother, and Amos Parsons knew Deke Grady used to be Pike's top gun."

"I remember Grady." Nate's jaw tightened, remembering Grady's curses as the noose went around his neck. "Why? What's Pike's got in mind?"

Pierce shifted uncomfortably. "He wants to drive folks off their land. Make 'em desperate enough to sell cheap. Then, he buys it all up. He paid us to cause trouble—burn a few barns, steal some horses, rough folks up."

Donovan exchanged a glance with Nate. "And what about Faith's ranch? Is that part of the plan?"

Sterling's eyes darted to the side. "Yeah. Pike's got his eye on her place, too. Figured if we caused enough trouble, she'd have to sell. But I swear, I ain't done nothing like tear up her storeroom or steal the bull. They just had me watchin'—and Amos is the one with the knife."

A brief memory of the mixed-race man in Royce's saloon surfaced, and Nate recalled the wicked-looking knife at his hip. He tightened his grip on Pierce.

"You're going to help us, Pierce—or so help me, you'll regret the day you were born."

"Help you how?"

Nate released the man, pinning him with an intense glare. "Tell me everything you know about Pike. Where's he hiding out?"

Sterling swallowed hard, his hands shaking. "There's an abandoned cabin up in the foothills outside town, but he don't stay there all the time. Mostly keeps weapons and supplies there."

"Where?"

"Due east, up that small range near the abandoned mine, right near a stand of cedars," Sterling answered. "It ain't hard to find. He sometimes meets some other man from Niobrara there. I ain't never met him, but I reckon they work together. That's all I know, I swear!"

Motioning Jed to bring the roan back, Nate shoved Pierce toward his horse. "Get outta here, Pierce—and don't let me catch you causin' trouble again."

Peirce scrambled onto his horse, casting one last fearful glance at Nate and Donovan before galloping away.

"Do you really think it's wise to let him leave, Nate?" Faith approached, her eyes filled with concern. "Shouldn't we take him to Sheriff Talbot?"

Before Nate could answer, Donovan snorted. "Not much help there, but I'm not sure we shoulda let him go free."

"Won't Pierce tell the gang we know about them?" Faith asked, twisting her hands together.

Nate turned to her, his expression softening. "Not if he wants to save his own skin. You were right, Faith. I'm thinkin' the man Pierce mentioned was meeting with Pike might be Gideon Hart. Provin' it won't be easy, though, and telling Talbot might tip our hand before we know enough."

"So, what are you going to do?" Faith's green eyes lingered on his.

A strange jolt shot through Nate. *When a man takes time to know her, Faith Shaw is a right pretty woman.* "I'm gonna clean up this gang once and for all. Pike won't get away with this again."

Faith placed a gentle hand on Nate's sleeve. "Just be careful, Nate. We don't need anyone else getting hurt."

Nate felt a small smile tug at his lips. "Don't worry, Faith. I'll make sure this ends once and for all."

***

Foothills near Niobrara

After leaving Faith's ranch, Nate went home to get some supplies. Travis showed up just as Nate was preparing to leave, full of his own plans for vengeance.

"I'm going after that gang, Sheriff Nate, no matter what you say," the young man declared, his jaw set with determination. "If Pike killed my pa, he's gonna pay."

Nate sighed, rubbing the back of his neck. "Travis, this ain't a game. These men are dangerous. If they killed your pa, they won't hesitate to do the same to you."

"That's exactly why I have to go." Travis's eyes blazed with anger and pain. "Pa was a good man, and they murdered him. I can't sit around and do nothing."

Nate studied the young man before him. Travis had always been headstrong, just like his father. Barrett had been a good friend, and his death had hit Nate hard. He understood the need for justice, but he also knew the danger.

"Listen, Travis," Nate began, placing a hand on Travis's arm. "I understand, but going after any gang alone is foolhardy. You need to think this through."

Travis shook his head. "I ain't thought about nothin' else since the day Pa died. I owe it to him to make sure those men pay."

Seeing the resolve in Travis's brown eyes, Nate realized there'd be no talking him out of it. *He's too much like his father.*

"All right, but you can't go off alone. Understand?"

Travis nodded, a flicker of relief crossing his face. "Yes, sir." Despite his show of bravado, Nate suspected the youth had come here hoping for help.

As Nate saddled Henry, he told Travis his plans to visit the cabin Pierce had mentioned. "I don't know what we'll find, but it gives us a place to start."

As they rode toward the foothills, the tension between them eased slightly. Nate knew this was about more than just revenge for Travis; it was about finding a way to move ahead without Barrett, to prove he'd done his best to find justice for his pa.

"Your pa would be proud of you, you know," Nate said quietly.

Travis shot him a surprised glance. "You think so?"

Nate nodded. "Barrett always talked about how strong you were, how you never gave up. You're a lot like him."

"Thanks, Sheriff Nate." Travis's expression softened. "It means a lot to hear you say that."

They rode in silence after that, speaking only after they'd passed the abandoned mine and dismounted to continue on foot. They'd tied Henry and Travis's mount, Dusty, to an oak halfway up the trail. Cedar perfumed the air as they followed Pierce's directions.

Nate and Travis moved swiftly through the dense underbrush, rifles slung over their shoulders. The cabin was exactly where Pierce had said it'd be, a pile of rotting boards half-sunk into the hillside, covered in brambles and vines. Crows sailed through holes in the roof, cawing as they wheeled across the sky.

Travis spotted it first. "There it is." He spoke in little more than a whisper, though they'd seen no sign of activity.

The sun slanted over the top of the ridge, sending deep shadows into the valleys. If they didn't hurry, it would be full dark as they made the trek back down the mountain. Nate scanned the clearing. No guards. No movement. Just the wind brushing through the trees as though whispering a warning.

"They aren't expecting anyone to find this place."

Travis snorted. "Or they're too cocky to care."

The weathered, tumble-down pile of lumber loomed ahead, settling into ruin.

"Looks like a stiff wind might knock it down," Nate whispered as they approached cautiously. "But ain't that a nice, shiny lock on the door?"

He lifted a boot and kicked in the door. The wood splintered, and the hasp of the lock snapped away from the hinges.

"Let's have a look inside."

Chapter Fourteen

After Nate kicked the door, Travis followed him into one big room; dust swirled up in a choking cloud, and spiderwebs dangled from the rotting beams. A heavy odor of mold, mouse droppings, and stale ash sent Travis into a coughing fit as they eased around the shattered door.

In the middle of the room, a rough-hewn table held a lamp, a three-legged chair shoved halfway underneath. Wooden crates were stacked high against the back wall, covered in burlap.

Nate pulled off the tarp, filling the air with dust, then pulled one of the crates from the stack. "It's heavy. Wonder what they're hiding?"

"Guess we'll see." Travis cracked the crate open with the butt of his rifle. "Look at that!"

Rifles. Ammunition. Enough firepower to hold the town hostage twice over.

Nate pried open a few more crates, speechless at the sight of gleaming Winchesters and box after box of cartridges.

Where did Pike get all this? And how big does the Coyote Clan plan to get?

"What now?" Travis asked. In the murky light, he looked younger, less certain than back at the ranch.

Nate glanced around, his eyes falling on the lamp atop the broken-down table. Picking it up, he pulled off the globe and poured the lamp oil over a couple of the crates, dousing them until the oil ran out.

"Now, we light it up and run like hell." He pulled a match from his shirt pocket, struck it across the sole of his boot, and held it to an oil-soaked crate.

The oil caught fast. Flames licked up the tinder-dry walls, devouring rotten wood and weapons alike. Nate and Travis hurried outside as thick plumes of black smoke curled into the sky. A pungent odor filled the air as those gleaming rifles melted, bullets exploding with small pops.

What a waste.

Travis glanced over his shoulder as they retreated. "It won't be enough," he said, shaking his head. "You know that."

"It's a start."

"A start? They killed Pa! We gotta do more." Travis's voice cracked. In the flickering light from the fire, his eyes glowed. "We should go after Pike. Tonight. Track him down and put a bullet in his skull—you gotta do *something*!"

"I *am* doing something." Nate gave the fire one more glance, then headed further into the scrub brush. "We've cut off some of their supplies, maybe slowed 'em down. That's the best we can do right now."

"It's not enough!"

The words hung heavy in the air. Nate saw the fury in Travis's face, the desperation. It was like looking into a mirror from years ago, before he'd hung up his guns, before the ranch, before he'd learned the cost of revenge.

Too high a price.

"I know what you're feeling," Nate said quietly. "I've felt it. I've lived it. But if you go after him now, you'll die—or worse, you'll lose everything you care about. I lost my wife, years with my boy, chasing after Pike's gang."

Travis clenched his jaw and looked away. "I don't care."

"You will," Nate said, "one day."

They hid in silence atop the ridge as the shack collapsed with a final groan of timber and flames. Sparks flew into the air, sailing up against the dark blue of the sky, as they turned and walked back to the horses. The sun had dropped behind the hills; black shadows covered the trail, but the faint glow of the smoldering fire behind them helped light the way.

Thankfully, they hadn't encountered any members of the Coyote Clan. Nate didn't trust the murderous scowl on Travis's face, the tight grip on his Remington.

Travis didn't speak again. When they neared town, Barrett's son headed in the opposite direction without even a good night.

The youth's silence worried Nate more than he cared to admit. Travis was like a powder keg: one spark, and he'd explode.

***

The ranch was quiet when Nate returned, but the air throbbed with tension. He'd left Donovan with Jed, unwilling to leave the boy alone after everything that had happened yesterday. As he rode past the house, he saw Jed pacing the porch; Donovan stood beside him, arms crossed, face grim.

The relieved grin that crossed Jed's face warmed Nate's heart. Deck gave a yip of welcome as Nate reined Henry to a halt and dropped wearily out of the saddle.

"Did you find the cabin?" Donovan asked.

Nate nodded. "We found the cabin and a stockpile of weapons. Nobody around. We torched everything, but this ain't the last we'll hear of 'em."

"I'll say it's not," Donovan muttered. "Got word from Lydia. Someone hit the store tonight. I was fixin' to ride back in, but didn't want to leave the boy alone."

"I told him I'd be all right," Jed added quickly, "but he said I'd have to ride in with him. That's when you rode up."

"Is Lydia hurt?" Nate felt the heat rise in his chest.

Donovan shook his head, already hurrying to ready his horse. "No, just shaken up. Simon Mitchell rode out to tell me." Donovan climbed into the saddle, obviously impatient to leave. "They smashed the windows, tore up the shelves. Sheriff's doing nothing, of course." He uttered a curse. "I've got to go."

"We're coming with you." Nate didn't hesitate. He mounted up again, held out a hand to Jed, and pulled the boy up behind him. "Deck, stay. Guard."

Deck moaned but sat back on his haunches, alert.

"You think it's that gang?" Jed's voice quavered.

"Could be," Nate answered absently, scolding himself as he wondered if Lydia's store had been vandalized because he and Travis dared fight back.

"Are you still gonna stop 'em, like you told Miz Shaw?"

"I plan to try."

***

Glass crunched under Nate's boots as he stepped inside the general store. Both plate-glass windows had been shattered; shelves and barrels had been overturned, scattering apples and crackers underfoot. The air was thick with the smells of vinegar, kerosene, and sawed wood.

Lydia knelt behind the counter, sweeping up shards with trembling hands.

"Lydia," Donovan said gently, pulling his wife up into his arms. "What happened?"

She looked up with red eyes and spotted Nate. "You growing moss out there yet, Nate?" she asked tremulously as she leaned in Donovan's arms.

"Not yet." Nate managed a small smile. "Did you see who they were, Lydia?"

"Not really. I'd just blown out the lamp when two men shoved open the door. They wore masks. Did... this." She waved around. "How will I ever clean all this mess...?" She trembled as she surveyed the wreckage. "Donovan, what are we going to do?" she whispered, her voice barely audible over the crunch of glass underfoot as Jed walked inside to stand beside Nate.

Donovan wrapped an arm around her shoulders, pulling her close. "We'll get through this, Lydia. We always do."

"But look at this place—it's ruined!" She shook her head, tears welling up in her eyes. "How will we ever recover?"

Donovan's grip tightened. "We'll rebuild. We've faced worse, haven't we?"

"You reckon we can?" Lydia searched his face.

"I know it." He nodded firmly. "We have each other, and that's all that matters."

She took a deep breath and let it out slowly. "You're right. We'll get through this. Together."

Donovan kissed her forehead. "That's my girl. Now, let's start cleaning up. One step at a time."

Lydia nodded, a small smile breaking through her tears. "One step at a time."

"Jed and I can help," Nate said. "What I want to know is, what did Sheriff Talbot have to say about this?"

"Was he here?" Donovan asked his wife. "Simon Mitchell said he stopped by the jail on the way out of town."

A look of disdain crossed Lydia's face, her lips pursed like she'd been sucking lemons. "Useless," she spat. "I had Royce go knock on the jail door, too. When the sheriff came, he said he'd 'look into it.'"

"Sounds like what I'd expect from him. Well, guess the first thing we need to do is sweep up this glass. Jed, go find a broom. Donovan, if you've got plywood, we can board up those windows."

Not for the first time, Nate wondered if Talbot might be on Hart or Pike's payroll. *Maybe Faith is more right than she knows.*

Chapter Fifteen

Nate stepped carefully over the debris, making his way to where Lydia knelt near the wooden counter. She reached for the spoils of candy jars, her face pale. He crouched beside her, gently taking a handful of ruined licorice whips from her hands.

"Let me help you with that."

Lydia looked at him, her eyes filled with gratitude. "Thank you, Nate. I don't know what we'd do without friends like you."

He gave her a reassuring smile. "We'll get this place cleaned up in no time. Don't you worry. Me and the boy got nowhere else to be."

"He's the image of Etta." Lydia nodded toward Jed, who was stacking canned goods beneath a broken shelf. "Royce told me how he just showed up on your doorstep after all these years."

"It was a surprise, all right."

As the rhythm of sweeping and stacking made the destruction a little easier to bear, Nate's thoughts wandered to Faith. "You know, Miz Shaw is a really good person," he remarked. "Guess Donovan told you all the trouble she's been having. Seems a shame. I don't know her all that well yet, but she seems kind and generous."

Lydia nodded, her expression softening. "She really is. She used to come here once a week and we'd talk. She wanted to learn medicine and help people, but figured she'd never get the chance. Her future was building up the Shaw Ranch, making Caleb's life count for something."

Nate paused, surprised. "She's got a lot of work ahead of her."

"If anyone can do it, she can," Lydia said. "She's quiet, but strong. She helped me when I was sick last winter. Didn't ask for a thing. Came every day, even with her own work piling up."

Nate felt something shift inside him. Respect for Faith Shaw, yes, but more than that, a yearning to understand her, to protect her. "She seems strong," he said, "but she's scared, too."

Lydia nodded slowly.

They worked quietly for a while, accompanied by the soft rustle of brooms and hammering from outside, where Donovan was boarding up the windows.

Finally, Lydia spoke again. "It's been hard for Faith since Caleb died. I don't know how she's managed. I can't imagine what either of us would do without Donovan."

Nate's heart ached for Faith, too, losing her husband. Even though he and Etta hadn't parted on the best of terms, they'd been in love once. He'd be lying if he said he hadn't had to blink away tears when Jed talked about her death.

As he swept the floor, Nate's mind kept drifting back to Faith's quiet strength. Her kindness. The concern she'd shown when she'd told him not to get hurt. He didn't know what tomorrow would bring, but tonight, he let himself think of what might be if they could end this uncertainty plaguing the town.

Lydia was arranging bolts of fabric, folding them to place on a shelf, when her voice broke into his musings. "You know, Donovan always says that, as long as we have each other, we can get through anything."

"He's right. We'll get through this, Lydia, and we'll be stronger for it."

She gave him a small, sad smile. "I hope so, Nate. I really do."

Once the last of the debris had been cleared away, Lydia looked around the store, her expression filled with determination. "We'll make this place better than it was before," she declared.

Donovan came inside, and Lydia sagged into his rugged arms.

"Let's get to bed. You're dead on your feet."

"Looks like Jed's already asleep." Chuckling, Nate pointed to his son, who had curled up like a puppy on the floor, his head resting against a saddle. "C'mon, son." He nudged the boy and helped him to his feet. "We might make it back to the ranch before the sun comes up."

Before long, they were riding Henry back to the ranch under a sky full of stars, the wind cool against Nate's face. Jed leaned against his back, warm and solid.

It had been a hard couple of days, the kind Pa used to say tested a man to his limits. Still, the moon shone, big and yellow, over the ranch. That old moon had been rising a long time. It didn't look like it was going anywhere.

In that moment, for the first time in days, Nate felt something close to hope.

***

Niobrara

A few days later

The town was alive with the buzz of celebration: Niobrara's annual Harvest Festival. Faith walked through the crowd, smiling at the familiar faces of her neighbors. She and Caleb had always loved these town gatherings, a chance for everyone to come together and forget their troubles for a while.

Today, however, her mind was elsewhere.

She couldn't bring herself to focus on the laughter or the scent of baked goods that filled the air. She barely heard the loud pops coming from behind the livery, where men practiced their sharpshooting skills for prizes. Sticky-handed children raced by her, unheeded, their faces streaked with mud as women in their Sunday best gossiped from porches and rocking chairs.

In past years, Faith would've been with the women, helping with the meal the Ladies Aide prepared to raise funds for orphans.

If only I could turn back time...

Faith made her way to Lydia's store with a heavy heart. The day after all her troubles—Jackson, the storeroom, losing Brutus—Donovan had given her the terrible news about Lydia's store. Lydia had been struggling to keep the store afloat, and Faith wanted to offer her friend some comfort.

"Truth is," Donovan had shared, "we owe so much at the bank, we can't buy new stock. Now, we may have to close."

As she approached the store, Faith felt a prickling sensation on the back of her neck. Instinctively, she touched the gun holstered at her side, her fingers brushing the cold metal.

"Faith," a voice called out, and she turned to see Lydia in the doorway of the general store, her face etched with worry. "I'm so glad you're here."

Faith smiled, trying to mask her own anxiety. "I came to check on you. How are you holding up?"

Lydia sighed, her shoulders slumping. "It's been rough. I don't know how much longer I can keep this place open."

"You'll figure something out. You always do." Faith placed a reassuring hand on her friend's shoulder. Hoping to change the subject, she looked out at the crowd. "Can you believe the town council voted to hold the Harvest Festival after all the trouble we've had recently?"

"Donovan heard that Sheriff Talbot insisted." Lydia looked around with a listless expression on her face. "Mr. Hart even provided fireworks to set off tonight. Guess the council wants people to think nothing's wrong."

As they spoke, Faith's eyes continued to scan the crowd. That's when she saw a strange man standing a few feet away, watching her intently. He was tall and well-dressed, with an air of confidence that set her on edge.

She took a step back, her hand tightening around the grip of her gun. "Lydia? Do you recognize that man standing by the hitching post near the feed store—the one wearing a blue serge suit?"

"Where—? Oh... I think I've seen him around before..."

Just then, two dewy-eyed young women hurried into the general store.

"Looks like you have customers," Faith said. "I'll come back later." She squeezed her friend's arm and turned to find the stranger still staring boldly at her.

Just what do you want?

She forced herself to walk over and confront him. "Can I help you?" she asked, her voice steady despite the unease she felt.

The man smiled, a cryptic expression that made her skin crawl. "Miz Faith Shaw? I'm Jonathon Marshall, Gideon Hart's lawyer. I have something for you."

He handed her a thick manila envelope, which she took reluctantly.

"What's this?"

"It's a final offer from Mr. Hart—a *generous* one. If you sign now, you'll walk away with a fortune... and your life."

Faith's grip on the envelope tightened, her anger flaring. "I'm not interested in anything Gideon Hart has to offer. Or his threats, either."

The lawyer's smile faded, to be replaced by a look of pity. "I advise you to consider it carefully. Mr. Hart holds a lot of power. It would be unwise to go against him."

Faith's jaw clenched, but she forced herself to remain calm. "I'll look it over, but don't expect me to change my mind."

"Very well. I'll be in touch." Marshall nodded, the expression in his eyes unreadable.

As he walked away, Faith noticed Lydia watching the exchange with keen eyes. "What was that about?"

"He said he's Hart's lawyer. Probably thinks he can scare me into selling." Faith handed her the envelope. "Here—read it, if you like. I have no interest."

Lydia opened the envelope, and her eyes widened as she examined the papers within. "Faith, you need to read this. The railroad has plans for your ranch, and—" Lydia gasped. Her already pale cheeks grew whiter. "I can't believe—he wants the whole town for the railroad! We'll lose the store for sure!"

"Let me read that." Faith's heart sank as she read the fine print beside Lydia's trembling finger. The railroad would cut through her land, destroying everything she and Caleb had worked for. And it wasn't just her ranch at stake now; the entire town would be affected. Dozens of people like Lydia and Donovan would lose their livelihoods.

"We can't let this happen," Faith said firmly. "I don't care how much Hart offers. I'm not selling out. If he can't get my ranch, they can't lay tracks through town. My ranch stands in his way."

Lydia nodded, her expression determined. "We need to fight this, to get the town on our side."

"I'm going to find Nate Holt. He needs to know about this." Faith took a deep breath, strengthening her resolve. "If anyone will know how to fight this, it'll be him."

She left Lydia's store, her mind racing. A few days ago, Sterling Pierce had hinted that Owen Pike was the one pushing people off their land, and with this new information, she was more sure than ever that he and Hart were working together.

As she walked through the crowd, she felt the weight of the town's future on her shoulders. She had to find a way to stop Hart, to protect her home and the town. She refused to let anyone destroy everything she loved.

Faith found Nate near the edge of the crowd, talking to a group of townspeople. She waited until he finished, then approached him, her heart pounding. He hadn't seemed too willing to speak the last time she stopped him on the street.

Am I being too bold?

"Mr. Holt—Nate—I need to speak to you."

Chapter Sixteen

A short time earlier

The town was abuzz with the sounds of celebration, a rare sight—and one Nate usually avoided. He'd never been one for large gatherings, preferring the solitude of his ranch and the company of his horses.

But today was different; today, he was here for Jed.

Jed had never seen a town celebration before. Not once—not a fair, not a parade, not even a pie-eating contest—so when he'd looked up that morning with quiet hope in his eyes, Nate couldn't say no.

"I ain't never been to a Harvest Festival before," Jed had said wistfully after

Nate had explained why he didn't plan to visit town that day. "Ma didn't much like going places. Wonder what it's like?"

Just like that, Nate had changed his mind. He hadn't been around for Jed's first twelve years, and if his boy wanted to go to the celebration, Nate wouldn't deny him. The ear-to-ear grin on Jed's face was reward enough.

The square had already been humming when they'd arrived. Chinese lanterns dangled from lines strung between buildings, swaying in the breeze. From the bandstand, fiddles and banjos twanged out lively music as people swarmed through the streets, gossiping around plank tables filled with hand-sewn goods, pies, cakes, jugs of lemonade, and dozens of other tempting wares. Jed's eyes grew wide, staring at everything like he was trying to memorize it.

Scents of freshly baked pies and the hog the Ladies Aide were roasting for their annual dinner perfumed the air. Cheerful bunting decorated the buildings, and Jed practically tripped over his feet, too captivated to watch where he walked.

A group of boys about Jed's age raced up. "Hey, wanna play a game of baseball?"

"Can I, Pa?"

Nate shooed him away. "Sure, go enjoy yourself."

Jed's face lit up, and he raced away.

Satisfaction welled in Nate's heart. Jed had been through so much; he deserved this moment of joy.

Even so, as Nate wandered through the crowd, he couldn't shake a familiar sense of unease. He'd always been that way in large gatherings, and today was no exception. When he found himself probing the scene for trouble, he noticed Faith weaving through the crowd—heading straight for him. A tight, anxious gleam filled her eyes, and her hands clenched a brown envelope.

"Mr. Holt—Nate—I need to speak to you," she said urgently. "Please."

"What's wrong?"

She handed him the envelope. "Read this. Gideon Hart's lawyer handed it to me today."

He pulled out the documents and read their contents, growing more indignant with each word he read.

"We can't let this happen," he said finally. "Hart will destroy the whole town, and he might be doing it with Pike's help. You heard Pierce say that Pike wants to run you off the ranch."

"I know," Faith replied, biting her lip, "but what can we do? How can we fight them—either of them?"

Nate grinned. "With a little help from our friends, I reckon."

The fiddler began a lively tune, almost too loud to hear a person think. "Let's step behind the church. Should be a little quieter there."

They'd only made it a few steps when Jed ran up, breathless and flushed. He stopped short, glanced at Faith curiously, then turned to Nate. "Is everything all right, Pa? Am I interrupting?"

Nate hesitated.

Faith looked at Jed, then back at him. "I know you told me this is your son, Nate, but we haven't been introduced properly. I'm Faith Shaw, your neighbor."

"This is my son, Jed." Nate placed a hand on Jed's shoulder.

Faith softened a little. "I saw you playing baseball. You're a fast runner."

Jed blinked, then ducked his head, a shy smile tugging at his mouth. "Thanks, Miz Shaw." Looked like Jed thought she might be special, too.

And what put that idea into my head?

"Everything's fine, son. We were just talking. Did you want something?"

"Ben, the boy who asked me to play, wanted to know if I can go look at his pony."

"Sure, go enjoy yourself. Make sure you get back for the hog roast."

Jed hesitated, then nodded and ran off, glancing back once before disappearing into a group of boys waiting for him.

Once Jed was out of earshot, Faith said, "He seems like a fine boy. Caleb and I were never so blessed."

"I always wanted a young'un," Nate leaned back against the warm bricks of the church's chimney. "Not sure what Etta thought early on." After a bitter laugh, he found himself sharing more than he had with anyone before, even Barrett. "Later, after I'd spent years chasing men like Pike, she couldn't take it. She left, said I was poisoned... and maybe she was right. I never even knew we had a son until he showed up on my doorstep."

"Your wife? Is she—"

Nate shook his head. "Dead, or I might never have known the boy. When he got here, he hated me." Pain settled in his gut, regrets about all the years of Jed's childhood he'd missed. Despite Jed's smile and good mood today, Nate knew the hurt must still fester.

We might still have rocky days ahead.

"Apparently, his ma bad-mouthed me every chance she got. Reckon I earned that reputation, though. Etta said I put bein' a lawman ahead of bein' a husband. She couldn't ever forgive that."

Suddenly, the jolly music drifting from the bandstand seemed out of place somehow.

Faith stepped closer, her green eyes filled with compassion. "You can't blame yourself for everything. Jed's here now, smiling. That's not hate—and no matter how his mother felt, it looks like he's willing to forgive the past."

She reached out, her fingers brushing his.

"You're here for him now," she said. "That's what matters."

"I don't know if I can be the pa he needs." Nate looked at her then, really looked; he caught the fire in those emerald eyes, the firm tilt of her chin. Stubbornness but warmth. Now, he realized that Faith Shaw had more grit than a dozen men he knew.

A sight prettier, too.

"You're trying," she replied. "That's more than most."

The moment stretched between them. Faith's hand lingered near Nate's, and something tugged at him. He couldn't say what he felt. Hope, maybe, or the ache of wanting. His breath hitched as their fingers brushed again.

He leaned in, just a little. She did too. The air between them charged, fragile, and electric. Filled with promise…

Crack!

A gunshot cracked through the air like a lightning strike, slicing the warm October afternoon in two. The fiddle and banjo screeched a sour chord and fell silent as the crowd froze for a breathless second.

Then, the screaming began. Children bolted from play, parents grabbed them mid-run, and the scent of popcorn and cider was drowned by gun smoke and panic.

Nate spun, instinctively pulling Faith behind the church wall. His hand went to the Colt at his hip, but it wasn't enough. Not for this. Whatever was happening had been planned to cause the most harm. To destroy the peaceful afternoon.

"Who—what's going on?" Faith clutched his sleeve so hard that he winced.

Nate peeked around the corner of the church to see smoke curling upward from the now-abandoned bandstand. The prized centerpiece of the town's celebration now stood in shambles, its wooden frame scorched, red-white-and-blue bunting fluttering in torn ribbons. Smoke billowed from a shattered lantern at its base, casting eerie shadows across the splintered stage.

The air pulsed with confusion and fear as townsfolk scrambled for cover, their festive clothes now streaked with dust and ash.

Three men with rifles stalked through the chaos, firing into the air as the crowd scattered. Their faces were masked, but their movements were precise and trained.

Faith gripped his arm. "We have to do something!"

"*I* will, but first, I get you safe," Nate said firmly. "There's a cellar beneath the church. Go—now."

She hesitated, searching his face. "I'm a good shot. Let me help."

Nate shook his head, feeling himself pulled in a dozen directions at once. "I need to find Jed. Then, I'll deal with those men. Don't let them find you."

She nodded and bit her lip. "Be careful," she whispered, then slipped down the church's cellar door like a shadow.

Nate watched her hide, then spun toward an alley between storefronts, his heart pounding.

I've got to find my boy!

Then, he heard a loud, unmistakable voice, one he'd have known anywhere.

"Sheriff Holt! We meet again—but this time, I'm going to win!"

Owen Pike had made his move, and now, everything was on the line.

Chapter Seventeen

Faith crouched behind a stack of crates in the damp cellar beneath the church, feeling like a cornered mouse. The wood felt splintery beneath her palms, and the scent of spilled lamp oil and musty potatoes filled her lungs with every shallow gasp, her body rigid with tension.

I hate hiding.

Nate had insisted, however, his voice low and urgent, his hand gripping her arm. Every instinct screamed to run, to fight, to find Nate and stand beside him. But he'd looked her in the eye—fierce, protective—as he said, "Go—now."

So I obeyed.

It wasn't in her nature to stand back from a fight, but she trusted Nate. Maybe almost as much as she once trusted Caleb.

Above her, muffled gunshots, screams, the crackle of flames. Glass shattered. Wood splintered. She waited. Counted heartbeats. Tried to listen past the ringing in her ears. It seemed to go on forever.

Then, silence: thick and ominous, like the lull before a storm breaks again.

No more gunfire. No more shouting. Just the faint creak of wood and the low moan of wind and distant thud of hoofbeats.

Faith rose slowly, climbed the short ladder, and pushed open the cellar door. It thumped against the side of the church. She blinked in the sunlight like a mouse coming out of a hole.

Without the gunfire and screams, the town was quiet in the strangest way. Not peaceful, but she sensed no danger. Pulling her revolver from the holster, she crept cautiously around the church, then gasped.

The Gold Dust's windows were shattered, smashed kegs and bottles dripping whiskey and beer into puddles on the boardwalk. Royce Tate came out with a broom, shaking his head, but didn't seem to notice her.

Smoke hung low over the center of town, curling around overturned tables. The bandstand supports smoldered, its torn bunting fluttering like wisps of charred paper. The scent of lemonade and roasted pork had given way to ash and gunpowder.

Faith's stomach twisted as she stepped carefully over smashed bits of pie, a trampled rag doll, and spent bullet casings.

She moved cautiously, searching for movement. No sign of the outlaws. No bodies. No blood smeared the dirt. Just destruction, senseless violence.

Faith's pulse quickened. If Pike had ordered this rampage, he hadn't come to kill; he'd come to show his power. To remind them he was watching. That he could reach them anytime.

Now, she began to understand why everyone spoke of the outlaw in fearful whispers.

She turned down the alley behind the general store. *Poor Lydia!* Barrels of apples were overturned, their contents stomped into mush. Brooms had been snapped in two, and tar smeared the windows in the double doors. There was no sign of Lydia or Donovan; the townspeople, they were probably cowering inside, terrified.

Faith emerged from the alley, slipping in a mix of apple pie and lamp oil. The town she'd known, where she bought thread from Lydia and traded eggs with Alice McCleary, appeared gutted. Doors hung loose on hinges. A buggy lay overturned in the street, wheels spinning lazily.

She rounded the corner past the general store and froze as relief shot through her, weakening her knees.

Nate crouched beside Jed, one hand on the boy's shoulder, the other gripping his Colt.

She opened her mouth to speak, but lost whatever thought she'd had as she saw the range of emotions playing across his weathered face. Grief in his blue eyes as he looked only at Jed, a stern crimping of his lips.

Of course his only thoughts were for his child. As they should be.

Then, Nate looked up, eyes locked onto hers. Relief flickered across his face, followed by something harder. Resolve? Anger?

Jed's pale face was streaked with soot, but his chin lifted like he was trying not to cry. Again. His nose dripped, and tears glistened on his cheeks.

"Jed? Are you all right?" Faith stepped forward, her voice barely above a whisper. She knelt beside him, brushing dirt from a torn sleeve. "Are you hurt?"

"I'm okay," he said, voice thin. "I saw 'em coming. Me and the other boys ran and hid." Jed shook his head, but his eyes darted toward the smoldering remains of the bandstand. He swiped an arm across a tear-streaked face, smearing dirt and snot.

"You're safe now," she said gently, hoping Nate would take her words to heart, too. "That's what matters."

Jed nodded, swallowing hard. "They didn't shoot anybody, just broke stuff and started fires. Why, Pa?"

"Well, son, think of it as a warning. Remember we talked about Owen Pike and his gang?" When the boy nodded, Nate stood, his jaw tight as he scanned the horizon. "He wants us to know he's back, that whatever he's after, we best give it to him or suffer the consequences." Reaching down to help Jed to his feet, he said, "We need to go home." His voice was low, but firm. "Faith, we'll talk soon. For now, let's get your horse, and we'll see you home safe."

Faith met his gaze, understanding that Nate's apparent calm was for Jed's benefit, to minimize his fright. There would be enough time later to figure out a plan.

"I'd appreciate that." She reached out for Jed's hand, surprised when he took it.

Together, they headed toward the livery, past the wreckage of the town, where people were slowly coming out to survey the damage. Strangely, out of everyone they passed along the way, Sheriff Talbot and Gideon Hart were noticeably absent.

"You'd think the sheriff would be out here, rounding up a posse," she murmured. "I saw no one trying to stop the gang."

Nate gave a humorless laugh. "Not strange at all."

Something in his voice chilled Faith's blood. *This is only the beginning.*

***

Shaw Ranch

Three days passed. The cattle grazed calmly, although there was still no sign of Brutus. Even so, tension tightened like baling wire pulled taut around her chest. She woke at night, breathing hard, twisted in the sheets as she fought imaginary dangers. Each morning, she got up and, aided by Donovan, tried to get through the day.

The sun was low when Faith rode into the yard on the fourth evening, Delilah lathered, her shoulders aching from a long day checking the north fence line. A few rails had been split clean through—likely deliberately—and Faith had spent hours hauling up replacements from the barn. Dust clung to her skin, and the scent of sawdust and sweat followed her as she dismounted. It took a few minutes to unsaddle Delilah and give her a cursory rubdown.

Faith was halfway to the porch when she saw him.

She stiffened, every muscle taut as a bowstring. The man before her was tall and gaunt, his face a map of old scars and fresh malice. His bottomless black eyes locked on hers with a predatory gleam. She could see the dark stubble on his chin, and a chill crawled up her spine at his presence.

He leaned against the porch post, arms crossed, hat tipped low. He wasn't from town. Faith would've remembered the sharp cut of his coat, the polished boots, the way he held himself like he owned the land he stood on.

Her hand went instinctively to the revolver in her holster.

"You're Faith Shaw," he said, voice smooth as creek stone.

She didn't answer. Just kept walking slowly, deliberately, until she reached the porch steps.

"We haven't met. My name's Owen Pike." He straightened, stepping forward, reached out a hand she refused to touch. "I believe you're acquainted with my friend, Gideon Hart." His voice was smooth, almost mocking, as though relishing the terror he inspired.

Faith forced herself to stand tall, though her knees threatened to buckle. "I don't care who you're friends with. You're trespassing." Her voice was steady, despite the panic clawing at her throat.

A cold smile twisted Pike's lips. "Gideon's made a generous offer on this ranch. Too generous, in my opinion, considering the state of things. He told me you keep stalling, refusing to sell. That don't seem very neighborly."

"I'm not selling." Faith crossed her arms, hiding the tremor in her hands. She'd left Donovon and Mark checking the rest of fence, so if Pike wanted to kill her, there was no one here to stop him. "Not to you. Not to Gideon Hart. Not to anyone. Now, please leave my ranch."

Pike's eyes narrowed, and for a moment, Faith saw the madness lurking behind them. "You see, Miz Shaw, that's the problem. You're interfering with a lot of plans. Hart doesn't like being ignored. If you keep refusing, things will get worse—for you *and* your friends. Remember what happened at the Harvest Festival?"

A cold wave of dread washed over Faith. She remembered the chaos, the gunshots, the screaming children, the flames licking up the bandstand. Her breath caught, and she struggled to keep her voice from shaking. "Are you threatening me?"

Pike sat down in her rocking chair, sprawling like a king surveying his kingdom. One boot propped on the railing, his hat tipped back, he looked her over with lazy confidence. "You can take it as a threat if you like. I think of it more like a business arrangement. Sell us your ranch, and we'll spare your life. Surely you haven't forgotten your dear departed husband, have you?"

Realization hit her like a bullet. *Caleb!*

Faith stepped closer, rage and terror warring inside. "Did you murder my husband? If you did, I'll—" Her voice broke, fury burning so hot she could scarcely breathe.

Pike leaned forward, feet thudding on the porch. "You'll *what*?" he sneered. "I know nothing about your husband's death, but you saw what happened in town. As you can see, the Coyote Clan"—he rose to his full height, looming over her, blocking out the sunlight—"gives fair warning about what could happen."

Faith's heart pounded so loud she was almost shocked Pike couldn't hear it, but she forced herself to meet his gaze, refusing to let him see her fear. "You didn't shoot anyone. You didn't even hurt a dog. That wasn't a warning," she retorted. "That was all just show."

Pike's eyes darkened, and the air between them seemed to thicken. "You think I won't go further?"

"I think you want me to believe you will," Faith replied, but her show of bravado felt paper-thin.

He leaned in, close enough that she smelled the whiskey on his foul breath and saw the madness flickering in his soulless eyes. "I don't bluff, Miz Shaw. Sell the ranch, or watch everything you care about burn to the ground."

Faith stood her ground, but in that moment, she knew Owen Pike was capable of anything; she and everyone she loved was in danger. As he rode away, Faith crumpled to the porch, her legs too shaky to hold her up, and knowing in her heart the worst was yet to come.

Chapter Eighteen

Faith didn't sleep that night. Wind howled through the trees, and every creak of the house settling sounded like footsteps. She sat by the window, a rifle across her lap, watching the horizon for riders coming to force her to leave.

None came.

The gray dawn rose slowly, like the day didn't want to wake up. Faith stood at the edge of the porch, her fingers wrapped around a tin mug of coffee gone cold. The rifle leaned against the wall behind her, where she'd laid it a few hours ago.

She watched the pasture, the way the mist clung to the grass like fairy breath. Delilah grazed peacefully near the fence, untouched by Pike's visit the day before. Faith envied the mare's ability to think only of comfort, fresh grass to graze, the sun on their withers. To move on, come what may.

Pike's voice still echoed in Faith's head. Right before he'd mounted a black stallion and left yesterday, he'd leered and said, "You've had your chance, Miz Shaw. Even the mighty Nate Holt can't help you. We *will* have this land."

She'd wanted to strangle him, but her anger wasn't enough—men like Pike didn't come to bargain; they came to take, to maim, to kill.

She sipped the tepid, bitter coffee. This ranch had belonged to Caleb's father, and his father before that. However, it wasn't only legacy that kept her rooted to this place; the soil itself held memories. She'd lain Caleb to rest on the east ridge, where first light hit in the morning. His parents were buried nearby.

With Donovan's help, she'd built this place back up. They'd shingled the barn roof after a bad winter storm. Nursed cattle through the drought. Paid the liens off, one by one, even when it had meant selling off the last of her mother's cherished jewelry.

This wasn't just land; it was proof that she could survive. That she could make something whole again.

Now, Pike and Hart wanted it for the railroad, but Faith knew what would happen if she sold: others would follow—the ranchers down by the creek, the old couple who ran the apple orchard. Even Donovan and Lydia would fold eventually, though they'd never admit it. Once one piece fell, the rest would tumble like fence posts in a flood, and it wouldn't be long before Niobrara echoed with the thunder of trains.

Perhaps that was what scared her most: not losing the ranch, but being the reason everyone else lost their homes.

Donovan walked from the barn to the house, footsteps slow and tired. Ever since the attack on Niobrara, he'd been sleeping at the ranch. Unable to reopen her store, Lydia had moved into the boarding house to help Sally Stewart cook and clean. It gave them a grub stake.

"Morning chores are done. Soon as Mark saddles up, he and Jackson plan to check the fences in the north pasture. I thought I'd ride to a few of the nearer ranches, check if anyone's seen Brutus."

"Is Jackson well enough to be working?"

Donovon shrugged and came to stand beside her, hands in his pockets, watching the same sunrise.

"He's young and tired of laying around."

"Make sure they're armed." Faith had lost no time telling her men about the encounter with Pike. As she expected, they'd been outraged on her behalf. Donovan had wanted to ride for the sheriff, but Faith told him not to bother. As long as Talbot wore a badge, nothing would be done to stop Pike.

"I keep thinking," she murmured thoughtfully, "if I sell to Pike, he'll take everyone else's home too. It'd give him a straight path to take over the town. Then again, maybe Pike would leave the others alone once he had my ranch. I'm the only way standing in his way—or so he says."

Donovan remained silent.

"I could take Hart's money. Move somewhere quiet and start over. Not have to worry about all this."

"You'd worry anyway," Donovan said, "and it wouldn't be where you and Caleb planted roots. You wouldn't be happy anywhere else."

She looked at him then. The lines around his eyes. The way his jaw clenched when he was trying not to say too much. Ever since Caleb's death, Donovan had put his heart and soul into the ranch. She relied on him as she would an older brother or uncle. For years now, he'd been her rock, the only one who understood the ranch and her. The only person she could tell how she honestly felt.

"I'm scared," she admitted, clamping the tin cup in her hands.

"I know."

"Not of Pike or Hart, though, not really. I'm scared that, by holding on so tight, I'll make everything worse for people like you and Lydia."

Donovan nodded. "That's the kind of fear that makes people noble. Or reckless."

Faith laughed, but it was hollow. "I don't feel noble."

"You feel responsible, Faith." He reached out to give her shoulder a brotherly pat. "It's kind of the same thing, and it's good—but don't make your choice based on what happens to other folks. We all must travel our own road."

"I know that." She swallowed hard. "I just keep thinking about the Thompsons. They're barely holding on to their orchard. If Hart or Pike pushes, they'll fold. The orchard will be buried under railroad tracks. The town will be gone."

"And you think selling will protect them?"

"I don't know. Maybe."

Donovan turned to her, his voice firmer now. "What if it tells Pike or Hart they can win if they push hard enough? Maybe what folks really need is someone to stand up for them."

Faith looked back at the pasture. Delilah had wandered closer to the fence, ears twitching at the sound of a distant cow lowing its displeasure. From the bunkhouse, she heard the rattle of harness, the good-natured voices of her ranch hands getting ready to ride out. Normal sounds.

If only it were an ordinary morning, not one where she needed to make such life-changing decisions.

The marmalade cat she'd named Sebastian came to purr along the railing. Faith put down the mug and pet his sleek fur. "I hate that it's all about money," she said, watching Sebastian preen under her touch, content with his lot in life. "That people think it's the answer to everything. That everything we build can be bought out from under us."

"It's not just money," Donovan argued. "It's power. It ain't just all about bringing the railroad or making more profit. Men like Hart want to see people suffer."

Faith felt tears sting her eyes, but she refused to let them fall.

Donovan reached for her hand, giving her a gentle squeeze, and stared straight into her eyes. "So don't sell," he said. "Not because you're worried about what will happen, but because you believe in what you and Caleb have built here. If you stand strong, others will too."

She gripped his hand tightly. "And if Pike comes back?"

"Then we meet him at the gate and make him leave."

Faith nodded, the fear still there, but something steadier beneath it: hope. With friends like Donovan and Nate Holt supporting her, it wasn't just her fight anymore.

I'm still here. I'm not alone.

And she wasn't leaving.

***

Niobrara

The saloon door creaked open, letting in a gust of wind that carried dust and the scent of stale tobacco. Nate stepped inside, jaw clenched, head throbbing. Royce's place was half full of ranch hands nursing beers, a few poker players hunched over cards, and the hum of low conversation. The familiar atmosphere should've been relaxing.

But Nate wasn't here for peace. He was here to keep from exploding from all the thoughts hammering in his mind.

He spotted Royce behind the bar, polishing a glass with a wary care that meant he'd already sensed Nate's mood from across the room. Nate gave him a nod and made his way over to lean against the mahogany bar.

"Whiskey."

Royce didn't ask questions. Just poured.

Nate took the glass and stared into it like it held answers to his most puzzling problem. Not Jed. Not Pike. Not the Coyote Clan.

Faith Shaw.

Today, she was the heaviest thought in his brain. When Faith stared at him with those green eyes, his heart melted like it had when he first courted Etta. But look how bad that had gone. Nate couldn't name the exact feeling that thrummed in his chest every time Faith looked at him—like he was something steady. Something good.

He *wanted* to be that for her, but the truth was, he didn't know if he could. Maybe he should find another woman, if not for himself, then for Jed. Maybe this time, he could learn to love a woman how she deserved.

Just now, though, with everything unraveling around them, Faith felt like a distraction. Part of him wanted to end it now. No explanations. Just walk away before she got hurt. Before he did.

But a small, stubborn voice inside him whispered at him to stay, to believe that maybe, just maybe, he could be something better. That, this time, he could have a good life.

Not until I take care of Pike.

He was halfway through his drink when he noticed Gideon Hart leaning against the end of the bar.

Nate's blood went hot, a flash-fire that roared up his spine and narrowed his vision to a red haze. His boots scraped hard against the floorboards as he turned, the sound sharp and sudden enough to make a few heads lift from their drinks.

Royce looked up from behind the bar, frowning, but Nate didn't stop.

Hart turned as Nate approached, an infuriating smirk curling his lips, like he'd been waiting for this moment. He leaned one elbow on the bar, casual as a man in his own parlor, and lifted his glass with a lazy flourish.

"Well, if it isn't the old sheriff," he drawled. "How's life treating you, Holt? Noticed you've been seen with the widow Shaw. Maybe you can convince her to sell her ranch. After all, it's not safe for a woman out there, alone."

"You're not welcome here," Nate growled, nostrils flaring. He planted his boots firmly, shoulders rising and falling with each breath.

Winking, Hart raised his glass again in mock salute. "Last I heard, this is Royce's place, not yours."

Nate's hand twitched near his belt, not quite reaching for his Colt, but close enough to make Royce shift behind the bar. "I know Pike's working for you," Nate said, ignoring the dismissive tilt of Hart's head as he held back a snarl.

Hart's smile didn't falter. "Pike does what he wants. I don't control him."

"You're lying." Nate stepped closer, his shadow stretching across Hart's face.

"Am I?" Hart leaned back against the bar, one hand still curled around his glass, the other resting near his coat pocket.

His posture was loose, but his eyes were sharp. "You've got a lot of anger, Nate. Maybe you should ask yourself why."

Nate's fist curled so tightly, his knuckles cracked. The muscles in his neck corded, and his lip curled just slightly. "You think this is a game?"

"You're in over your head, Holt, and going under for the third time."

Nate's hand shot forward to jab a finger hard against the chest of Hart's fine linen shirt. Hart didn't flinch, just looked down at the finger like it was a fly.

"Out—both of you," Royce barked suddenly, cracking through the standoff like a whip.

Nate turned, surprised, his hand still hovering mid-air. "Royce, he—"

"I said *out*." Royce stepped out from behind the bar, twelve-gauge resting in the crook of his arm. "I won't have blood on my floor today."

Hart stood slowly, brushing off his coat as though inconvenienced by a gust of wind. He straightened his collar, adjusted his cuffs, and sighed theatrically.

"Always a pleasure." He tipped his bowler hat to Royce, then to Nate. "Do give Miz Shaw my regards."

That did it.

Nate lunged, but Royce was already there, stepping between them with practiced speed, one hand firm on Nate's chest, the other tightening on the shotgun in his other hand.

"*Out*," Royce repeated, voice like iron, eyes as gray as flint.

Nate's eyes locked on Hart like he could burn a hole through him. Every muscle in his body screamed to punch Hart's smug face, but Royce didn't budge, and the room had gone silent. Every eye was on them.

Hart gave one last smirk and turned, sauntering out like he owned the town.

That might not be too far from the truth.

Nate stood there, heart pounding, jaw clenched so hard, it felt like his teeth might crack. But he kept his mouth shut, turned, and stalked after Hart.

Chapter Nineteen

The door slapped shut behind Nate as he stepped off the boardwalk, kicking up dust with every stride. Hart was nowhere to be seen. Good thing he'd crawled back under his rock somewhere, or Nate might have been tempted to end their argument in the worst way.

The setting sun cast shadows that stretched like spectral fingers across the street. Nate didn't know where he was headed, just away—away from Hart's smirk, away from Royce's shotgun, away from the urge to break something or hit somebody.

He was halfway to the edge of town when a noise lifted the hair on the back of his neck. Black shadows hovered beside the buildings; a chill wind shivered through his leather duster.

The livery, where he'd stabled Henry, was just ahead. He needed to ride, to burn off the fury still clawing at his ribs. The whiskey hadn't helped. Neither had Royce's dismissal. Gideon Hart's smirk was still etched behind his eyes like a brand.

Then, he heard it again.

Footsteps.

Light. Measured. Not something a man wanted to hear in the gloom of dusk—especially not behind him.

Nate stopped cold. His hand dropped to his belt, fingers brushing the worn grip of his Colt. Had Hart come back to fight, after all?

"Who's there?" he barked, spinning on his heel, raising his weapon. Squinting into the gloom, he saw, not Hart, but a paler face.

Sterling Pierce stood ten paces back, hands raised, palms open to the fading light. His coat flapped in the breeze, dust clinging to the hem. His gaunt face was drawn, eyes wary, like a man who'd seen too much and didn't trust what he saw now.

"Easy," he said soothingly. "I'm not here to fight."

Nate didn't lower his gun. "Then why are you following me?"

Sterling took a cautious step forward. "Can we talk?" Looking over his shoulder, he fidgeted. "Somewhere quiet where no one will see us?"

Nate's eyes narrowed. "You picked a bad time, Pierce."

"Maybe..." Sterling glanced toward the saloon down the street. Lamplight shone from the windows, the lively tinkle of the piano drifting out. "But I figured after what just happened in there, you might be ready to listen."

Nate's pulse still hammered with rage. "You saw that?"

"Guess everybody in the saloon saw," Sterling said. "If Tate hadn't stopped you, you'd have put Hart through a window."

"Should've."

Sterling just stood there warily, hands still raised. "I'm not here to defend him," he said. "I'm here because I'm tired."

"Tired," Nate repeated, voice flat as a dry creek bed. His unblinking eyes didn't soften. "Of what?"

Sterling's shoulders sagged beneath the worn canvas of his coat, and his hands, still raised, trembled slightly in the fading light. "Of the threats. The lies. Of watching good folks get trampled while Owen rides roughshod to get his own way."

Nate stowed his revolver in its holster, fingers flexing against the worn leather. The sky above them purpled deeper, clouds rolling low like a warning. "You work for him."

"Not anymore."

"That's awful convenient." Nate stepped forward, scanning Sterling's face for a lie, a twitch—or the truth.

Sterling didn't flinch, but he lowered his hands slowly, palms still open in surrender. "I'm not asking you to trust me, just to hear me out."

Nate's body coiled, as if bracing for a blow. Wind rustled through the trees, and somewhere behind them, a loose shutter whined on rusty hinges. A horse neighed from the livery, then a *thump* of wood against wood.

"Make it quick," Nate said finally.

Sterling exhaled, shoulders drooping further. He looked older in that moment, like the gravity of everything he'd done had settled into his bones. He glanced quickly over his shoulder, then moved in closer.

"Pike's not bluffing anymore," he murmured. "He's not just cutting fences or torching barns. He's making people disappear, and I want no part of it."

Nate's eyes stayed locked on Sterling's. "You expect me to believe you've grown a conscience?"

"I want out," Sterling insisted, "and I think you want this to end just as much as I do."

Nate didn't move.

"I want to help you stop Pike," Sterling said. "I know where he hides. I know who pays for his dirty work, who helped him escape from prison. I know what he's planning next. So far, I ain't done nothing that would get me hanged—jail maybe, but not the gallows—and, honest to God, I wanna stop before a hangman puts a noose around my neck."

Nate stared at him. Everything in him screamed not to trust this outlaw. But with everything he'd seen lately, he realized they didn't have time to wait for someone better to come along. "Why tell me?"

"Because you're the only one left who might actually *do* something," Sterling said, "and if I don't help, I got a feelin' I'll be the next to die."

Nate looked at the lines around Sterling's eyes. The way his coat hung loose on his frame. The tremor in his voice told Nate that he was scared.

He may be telling the truth.

"Fine," Nate said, stepping back. "I'll take your help—but if you cross me, so help me, you'll regret the day you tried."

"I won't," Sterling said. "I've got nowhere else to go. Give me some time, and I'll bring you something solid. If you need to find me, I've set up camp out past that abandoned way station on Simons Road."

Nate nodded and turned without another word, heading toward the livery.

The ride home was quiet. Nate's mind churned, replaying Sterling's words, but doubt invaded every thought. Could he trust a man who'd helped light the match to burn his barn? Or was this just another trap, a way to get close enough to strike the killing blow?

He reached the ranch with a scant hour of twilight left. The storm appeared to be sailing away with just a spatter of raindrops. "C'mon, Henry—let's check on the herd before we call it a night." Nate tugged the reins, guiding the patient gelding over the ridge. The cattle were blurred shapes across the pasture, some grazing, others settled for the coming night.

Then, he saw it.

Splintered fence posts—three in a row—cut clean through, the ends chipped and raw. Loose barbed wire coiled like a snake in the grass.

Nate swung down from the saddle, landing against the earth with a weight that matched the dread rising in his chest. He looped Henry's reins loosely to a fence rail still standing, then crouched low.

The cuts were too clean. Not the work of weather or wear.

Someone had been here. Recently.

He ran his hand along the grain, feeling the moisture clinging to the rough splinters. The soil around the base was churned up, fresh hoofprints pressed deep into the sod, wide and erratic. Whoever had come through hadn't cared enough to bother hiding their tracks.

Nate rose slowly, peering at the ground in the waning light. The prints led off toward the hills, weaving drunkenly through the brush. After checking the rounds in his Colt, he followed.

Weak sunlight spilled across the landscape in pale streaks, silvering the tops of rocks and casting long shadows through the scrub. The scent of juniper and dry grass tinged the night breeze. Crickets chirped in the distance, their rhythm steady, indifferent.

The trail climbed gradually, winding through a narrow pass where the rocks closed in tight. Nate moved carefully, slipping against loose scree, the occasional *snap* of a twig sounding unnaturally loud. He kept low, eyes sharp, ears tuned to every rustle—until he smelled something out of place.

Smoke.

A faint wisp, but not from a campfire. Bitter. Lingering. It curled into the air like a whisper, barely visible against the moonlit sky.

Nate paused, nostrils flaring. The wind shifted, carrying the scent stronger now: burnt wood, scorched earth, something darker beneath it. A scent he dreaded.

Death.

Chapter Twenty

Nate crested the next rise, then froze.

A burnt-out wagon lay upturned, its contents spilled, iron fittings warped in the heat, twisting like broken limbs. Barrels of flour and meal had cracked open. Charred clothes lay scattered over the ground, caught on bushes, household goods tossed about like child's toys.

As Nate approached, the acrid scent of burned wood and canvas stung his nose. Each breath tasted of soot and fear. He reached out, fingertips grazing the scorched edge of a wheel hub, not warm. Not fresh, but the fire had done its damage not long ago—enough time for the ashes to settle; recent enough that the smoke still lingered.

He crouched again, eyeing the debris with the precision of a man who'd seen too many things go wrong. A child's boot, half-buried in ash. A tin cup, dented and blackened. The remnants of a ledger, its curled pages fused together like dead leaves. Gold leaf spelled out *Titus Jenkins* on the book's cover.

Nate's stomach turned.

Titus had lived on a nearby ranch with his wife and two daughters. Nate remembered their youngest, Abby, chasing chickens outside the feed store, laughing so hard she hiccuped.

Where are they now?

Nate pressed his palm into the soil, studying the ground around the wagon. No drag marks. No footprints. No signs of struggle. Just absence. Silence.

Bile rose in his throat as he faced the grim truth.

Curls of smoke rose from the blackened frame as Nate stared at the wreckage. The lies around town had been simple: the Jenkins family had left to dodge taxes, to escape Hart's threats. Gone in the night. No one had questioned it.

That was the point, he realized. Hart only needed people to believe the story long enough for the evidence to rot. Long enough for the memory to fade.

The Jenkinses hadn't left; they'd been taken—and if Nate's suspicions were right, what remained of the Jenkins family was still in that wagon.

Nate rose slowly and glanced up the ravine walls, half expecting the glint of a rifle barrel in the dying light of gloaming. But there was nothing.

Just the hush of scorched earth and the whisper of a lie too big to ignore.

The wagon hadn't been abandoned in haste. It had been burned and hidden in plain sight. A grave with no headstone, no names, no mourning. Just ash and silence.

Horror pressed down on Nate's chest, making his breaths shallow. It wasn't just the deed itself, but the calculated precision. Jenkins may have been the first, but he wouldn't be the last.

Suddenly, Nate thought of Jed: young, curious, always wandering away from the ranch with Deck and a fishing pole. What if he'd stumbled upon this awful scene? His stomach twisted, pulse thudding in his ears.

Nate turned, stomping over the scorched soil. He glanced around again, looking for any clue pointing to who'd committed the crime—tracks, shell casings, a scrap of cloth. Nothing. Just the ruin. Just the remains of a family that had been murdered by greed.

The law wouldn't help. Talbot was a coward, and the town council was too cowed to risk their own necks. Nate knew that now.

If they wanted to survive, they'd have to move. Fast. Quiet. If Pike was willing to burn a family alive and bury the truth in a ravine, no one was safe.

Pierce had told the truth: Pike was making people disappear for good.

He's probably the one who killed Barrett, too.

How much had Sterling Pierce known about the Jenkin's family? Had he helped with the massacre? Maybe it was time to ask him why he was suddenly so eager to leave the gang.

Nate picked up the scorched ledger and put it in his saddlebag; perhaps Talbot would be *forced* to act if confronted with some concrete proof.

Nate didn't have the answers, but he vowed to find out. Perhaps Sterling could help provide clues to help them beat Pike. One thing was clear, though.

They were running out of time.

***

The pounding came long before dawn.

Nate jolted upright, heart thudding, reaching for the Colt on the table by his bed.

Jed stirred on the floor beside him, groggy and blinking. "What's wrong, Pa?" he asked as he sat up on the pallet.

"I don't know. Stay here." Nate grabbed a pair of pants and jerked them on over his union suit, pulling up suspenders as he hurried to the door.

Another round of sharp, insistent knocking—not the rhythm of a drunk or someone who meant harm; no, this was panic.

Nate swung the door open to find June on the porch, hair wild, eyes rimmed red.

"It's Travis," she gasped without preamble, almost falling into his arms. "He's gone, Sheriff Nate!"

Nate blinked. "Gone?"

"No one's seen him since last night. He didn't come home. I went out looking this morning, but…" She clenched his arms in a death-grip. "I'm frightened—it's not like him to just disappear!"

"No, it's not." Nate felt a chill settle in his chest. Travis wasn't the type to vanish; he was too protective of June. He thought of the Jenkinses' wagon. How far would Pike go to cover his schemes? What reason would he have to take Travis?

Unless the reckless boy has gone off on his own to find Barrett's killer…

Jed came into the front room, rubbing his eyes. "What happened?"

"Travis is missing." Already, Nate was pulling on his boots, strapping the holster around his waist. "When did you last see him?" He asked June.

June stepped back, voice low. "He went out riding after supper, said he wanted to check the fence near the river. No one's seen him since."

"That's where I'll start, then." Nate reached for the door. "June, would you mind staying here with Jed? If I'm not back near dusk, head over to Faith Shaw's. Tell her and Donovan what happened."

"I want to come, too," Jed said, wiping the sleep from his eyes.

"No," Nate answered more sharply than he'd intended, thinking of little Abby Jenkins. "It's too dangerous."

Jed frowned. "I've been practicing how to shoot. You know I have. I'm not a little kid anymore."

"You're staying here." Nate turned, jaw tight.

"But—"

"I said, *no!*" The word cracked through the room like a shot.

Jed flinched. June looked away.

It was the first time Nate had raised his voice to the boy. Not in frustration. Not for discipline.

In fear.

"I'm your pa," Nate said more softly, but no less firm. "Listen to me. You stay here with June. Don't leave this ranch."

Jed's face flushed, fists clenched at his sides. "You think I can't help you?"

"I *think* I don't want to bury *you* next."

Jed's eyes filled with tears, but he didn't speak. In his face, Nate saw the same things he'd felt at that age—anger, hurt, bruised pride—but beneath that, understanding and grudging acceptance.

He'd gotten through to Jed, as Nate's own pa had gotten through to him.

"We'll talk when I get back," Nate said, stepping onto the porch. "You take care of June."

He didn't wait for an answer as he went to saddle Henry.

The outskirts of town were quiet, morning mist clinging to the grass. Nate rode hard, studying the horizon, heart pounding with every hoofbeat. He passed the old Jenkins property, the scorched wagon still raw in his memory. Pike had removed them. Burned their wagon. Buried the truth.

Now, Travis was missing.

The Niobrara River came into view, winding slow and silver through the trees. Nate slowed Henry, eyeing along the riverbank. He'd been riding about half an hour when he came upon the horse.

A chestnut gelding, reins dragging, saddle empty.

Travis's horse, Dusty.

Nate dismounted and approached slowly. Dusty's nostrils flared, his ears twitching nervously as Nate ran a hand along his neck, murmuring.

The saddle was intact. No sign of a fall. No damaged tack. Nothing to show Travis had taken a tumble while riding along. No man lying in a ditch, wounded, unable to call for help.

Nate crouched, examining the ground. Tracks led away from the river, into the brush: two sets of clear boot prints. Then, abruptly, one pair of imprints stopped.

What were you following, Travis?

Nate followed the other set of tracks until they veered toward a cluster of rocks, then vanished, leaving something more ominous. His breath caught.

Blood.

Dark, dried, spattered across the stone. Not a man's lifeblood, but enough to show someone had been injured.

Nate looked around the area, heart hammering. A broken branch. Disturbed earth. A single bullet casing, glinting in the morning sunlight.

He picked it up, rolled it between his fingers. It was a .45 caliber, recently fired. Nate gripped it tight, knuckles white.

Seventeen years ago, the Coyote Clan had often left behind a clue: a single bullet, a taunt. Nate didn't need the reminder to get the message.

Travis had been taken.

Nate stood there for a long moment, wind rustling through the trees, the river whispering behind him. Weight settled on his shoulders, just as it had so many years before, when he'd risked everything to bring Pike to justice.

Barrett. Faith's husband. Jenkins. And now, Travis.

Shoving the casing into his coat pocket, Nate turned back toward Henry and Dusty. He had to get back, warn the others. Had to move, before Pike killed Travis, as he'd likely killed Barrett and the Jenkins family.

But something gnawed at him. A question.

Why take Travis?

Sure, he'd been determined to track down his pa's killer. Bull-headed, just like his father, stubborn and reckless. Even so, he was just a kid, not much of a threat.

Pike knew I'd come searching, he realized. *Knew I'd find his calling card.*

Nate looked along the tree line one last time. No movement. No sound. Just the hush of a place that had swallowed a man whole.

After tying Dusty's reins to the back of Henry's saddle, Nate rode hard back toward the ranch, the reins tight in his fists, the bullet casing burning a hole in his pocket.

When he rode into the barnyard, Jed's mouth opened wordlessly. His eyes flicked to Dusty's empty saddle, then to Nate's face, searching for something—answers, perhaps, reassurance, a comforting lie—but Nate had none to offer. The boy's silence was louder than any scream.

June had been pacing the porch. Like Jed, she stared at Travis's empty saddle. "Was he..." Her mouth couldn't seem to form the dreaded question.

"No, I didn't find him," Nate assured her, deciding to keep the fact that he'd seen blood to himself for now. "Looked like signs of a struggle, though. Reckon someone nabbed him." He dismounted and stepped heavily onto the porch, the bullet casing pressing against his ribs like a cold warning.

"What are you going to do?" June asked, clenching and unclenching her hands.

He turned and looked out across the yard, past the fence line, toward the hills that swallowed the river. Somewhere out there, Pike was waiting. Maybe laughing.

Nate felt an old, bitter rage stir in his chest. He'd buried too many good men. Seen too many families torn apart. And now, Travis, barely a man, full of fire... gone. Just like that. No warning. Just blood on the rocks and a casing in the dirt.

"You're gonna go after him, aren't you?" Jed whispered.

Nate didn't answer. From the fear etched across both faces, he knew he didn't have to.

"I want you two to come with me to town. You can stay with Lydia. Tell her what happened. I'm going to get together a search party." He gave June what he hoped was a reassuring smile. "We'll find Travis, don't you worry."

Pike had made his next move.

And Nate didn't plan to let him finish the game.

Chapter Twenty-One

The sun had already climbed high when Nate rode away from the ranch, heat pressing down. It was going to be another scorcher, but he didn't have time to wait for dusk. Travis was out there somewhere, hopefully still alive. If Pike had him, every second counted.

Nate went to the Gold Dust first. Royce had just unlocked the doors and pushed open the green curtains on the windows.

"You're out and about awful early," he said as Nate dismounted, tied Henry to a hitching post, and followed him into the dim saloon. "What's got you in a stew?"

"Travis has gone missing. June said he rode out last night and hasn't been seen since." Nate leaned against the bar while Royce poured them each a bracing cup of coffee. "I found his horse down by the river this morning. Blood on the rocks and a bullet casing—just like Pike used to leave."

Seventeen years ago, Royce had been in the posse tracking Pike. He knew the outlaw's tactics almost as well as Nate.

Royce shifted, wincing. "You think Pike has him? Maybe Travis saw something…"

"I'm guessing he was asking questions about his pa's death. He was stubborn. Bull-headed. Just like Barrett."

Royce looked away, jaw tight. "Barrett was a good man. If he learned about Pike escaping, he'd have tracked him to the ends of the earth."

"Travis inherited that fire. Looked like he might have been following someone near the river."

Nate took a gulp of coffee. "That's not all. Yesterday, I came across a burnt-out wagon in the ravine past my ranch. Remember Jenkins?"

"Titus? Sure. Word around town was, they left to keep from paying back taxes."

"Lies. What's left of Jenkins and his family are in that burned wagon, and I think Pike is behind it. I'm going after him."

Royce didn't hesitate or question. "Let me get Caesar from the livery, and I'll join you." He pulled the twelve-gauge from behind the bar, clapped an old slouch hat on his head, and headed out the door.

They rode together to Sterling's camp, a mile past the abandoned way station.. Nate didn't like trusting the outlaw, but he was running out of options. Sterling had a sharp eye and a quick trigger. That made him dangerous—but it also made him useful, especially since he'd worked with Pike.

Sterling was leaning against a tree, cleaning his revolver, when they arrived. He looked up, startled. "I haven't learned anything new ye—"

"Travis Rivers is missing." Nate didn't waste time in small talk. "Pike's probably behind it. I need your help *now*."

Sterling paled and holstered his revolver. "The deputy's son?"

"I found his horse. Some blood, but no body. Just a single casing."

"How can I help?"

"I want to find him before sundown."

Sterling nodded slowly. "All right, I think we can get to Pike's hideout before then." Sterling moved to a paint, tethered to a picket line. "Soon as I saddle up, we can ride."

Returning to the riverbank, they followed the tracks, Royce scanning the ground, Sterling watching the horizon. Nate kept his eyes on the trail, boot prints, broken branches, the occasional scuff in the dirt. He knew from experience that Pike was smart, but often careless—leaving signs of his passage, as though daring anyone to follow.

Of course, as Nate knew well, Pike was also unpredictable; he'd double back, bait traps, and leave false clues.

The trail led them west into a box canyon Nate recognized. The canyon was narrow and steep, a perfect place for an ambush. He slowed Henry, unease prickling at the back of his neck.

Royce rode up beside him. "You feel that?" he murmured.

"Yeah—like we're being watched."

Sterling kept quiet, looking along the rims overhead. He slowed his horse and whispered, "Last time I rode with the Coyotes, we hid out here. Can't say for sure he's here, but if I had to guess..." His voice petered out, and his face adopted a queasy expression.

Nate dismounted and motioned for the others to do the same. "We'll continue on foot. Spread out. Watch for any movement behind the rocks."

They moved slowly, rifles ready, boots careful on dry stone. The rocky walls loomed above, casting them into false twilight. Nate's heart thudded in his chest, every step like an omen of danger.

Out of nowhere, gunfire rained down from above, sharp, echoing, relentless. Bullets tore through the air, kicking up dust and chipping off stone.

Nate ducked behind a boulder, Royce beside him, as Sterling dove for cover across the way.

"It's an ambush!" Nate shouted.

"You don't sa—"

Suddenly, Royce grunted, his words cut short, and clutched his shoulder. Blood seeped through his plaid shirt, dark and fast.

"Royce!" Nate crawled to him, dragging him behind the rock. "Hold on!"

"Shoulder. Clean through, I think." Royce gritted his teeth as the blood drained from his face. "I'll live, but it hurts something fierce."

Peering around the rock, Nate saw at least four shooters, but he suspected more lurked in crevices. They were obviously outnumbered, and their attackers had the high ground and advantage of better cover.

Sterling fired back, quick and precise, then ducked as a bullet ricocheted off the stone near his head. "We're outgunned! What do you want to do, Holt?"

Nate's mind raced. Royce was injured; Travis was nowhere in sight... and now, Pike knew they were on his trail.

He glared at Sterling, suspicion flaring. "Did you know this was coming?"

Sterling's eyes flashed. "You're joking, right? Why in blazes would I walk into my own blasted trap?"

Nate didn't have time to process that now. He tore a strip from his shirt and pressed it to Royce's wound. "We've gotta make tracks."

Royce clutched his arm weakly. "Don't leave me."

"Not a chance."

Sterling laid down cover fire as Nate hauled Royce to his feet, slinging the man's arm over his shoulder. They moved quickly, ducking and weaving between rocks. Bullets chased them, snapping past their ears. The canyon mouth was a hundred yards away, but it felt more like miles.

Sterling fired again, then sprinted to join them. "Go! I've got the rear!"

They ran, Royce stumbling, Nate dragging him forward, lungs burning, legs screaming. The gunfire slowed. Pike's men weren't chasing; they didn't need to.

They'd made their point.

When they reached the horses, Nate practically threw Royce into the saddle. Sterling mounted fast, eyes still scanning the cliffs.

"Ride!" Nate shouted.

They galloped away, the canyon shrinking behind them, the echoes of gunfire fading into silence. They made it to a grove a few miles out, hidden by trees and brush. Nate dismounted, helped Royce down, and checked his shoulder. The wound was bad, but not fatal. He'd need stitching up, probably a few days' rest.

Sterling paced nearby, jaw tight. "It felt like Pike knew we were coming. His men were waiting."

Nate nodded. "Means someone's talking." He glared hard at Sterling. *I still haven't asked him about his part in what happened to Jenkins.* "You?"

"You think I'd want to get myself shot? Now that Pike's seen me with you, I've got a target on my back, too. I'm not a fool."

Nate continued to stare at Sterling, reluctant to trust a word he said. His hand hovered near his Colt, fingers twitching with the urge to act, but he held himself in.

"I think you used to ride with Pike. You know how he thinks." Nate's voice was low, rough as gravel, but steady. He took a step closer, boots crunching on brittle leaves, his shadow looming over Sterling in the dying light.

Sterling stepped forward, too, his breath visible in the cooling air. "And *I* think you're desperate enough to trust me, even if you hate it."

Nate didn't flinch. "I am."

They stared at each other, the tension thick as a storm cloud.

Royce groaned, shifting against the tree, his breath ragged. Nate knelt beside him, pieces of bark rough beneath his knees, and pressed a steadying hand to Royce's trembling shoulder. "You're all right. We'll get you patched up."

Royce nodded, eyes glassy. "Travis..."

"We'll find him," Nate promised, his voice hard as iron. He looked up, every sense straining for danger. The breeze picked up, carrying the scent of gunpowder and pine. Somewhere in the distance, a coyote yipped sharply.

The game had changed. Pike knew they were close

Then, mocking voice drifted on the wind, impossible to locate in the gathering gloom.

"You're too late, Holt. You'll never find him alive."

Chapter Twenty-Two

Faith was brushing Delilah down when she heard a horse gallop into the barnyard. Fast. Urgent. She turned just as Donovan reined in, kicking up dirt and pebbles. His face was pale beneath the trail grime, eyes wide and tormented.

"Faith," he gasped, sliding off the saddle. "Bad news."

She dropped the brush. "What happened?"

"Travis Rivers is missing."

The words hit like a slap. "Deputy Rivers' son?"

Donovan nodded, breath ragged. "He went out the other night to check fences. June, his sister, expected him by supper. He never came back."

"No one's seen him?"

"Not a sign, until June went to Nate's yesterday. Nate went right out, found Travis's horse, and signs of a struggle down by the river. Looked like someone took him." Donovan's jaw clenched. "Nate, Royce, and Sterling Pierce went after him. Thought maybe Pike's men had him. They ran into an ambush."

Faith's stomach dropped. The world tilted, just as it had the day Talbot had come to tell her Caleb had died. Words formed on her lips, but she had to swallow hard before she could speak them. "Is he—are they... hurt?"

"Mostly just scraped up and bruised, though Royce took a bullet through the shoulder. Nate managed to drag him out, but they barely made it. No sign of Travis."

She gripped the fence rail to steady herself as relief washed through her body. *No one is dead. Thank God.* "Where's Nate now?"

"Went back to his ranch after dropping Royce off at Doc's. Said he wanted to talk to you, so he's com—"

Faith shook her head, already reaching for the saddle blanket. "I'll go there."

The ride to Nate's ranch was a blur. She hadn't even bothered to saddle Delilah properly. She rode hard, recklessly, her heart pounding with every hoofbeat.

Her thoughts spun. Travis, Deputy Rivers' son, missing. Nate had mentioned that he feared the boy would try to avenge his pa's death. Nate and the men ambushed.

Wait... Sterling Pierce? Isn't he the one Nate found spying on my ranch?

Why would Nate take an outlaw along to search for Travis?

By the time she reached the gate, the sun had dipped nearly to the horizon, casting long shadows across the parched earth.

The wind had picked up, carrying the scent of dust, sagebrush, and something sharper, like charred wood. Donovan's news still echoed in her brain like a drumbeat of doom.

Nate was on the porch, slouched in a battered rocking chair like he'd been dropped there. He looked up as she dismounted, his eyes narrowing against the slanted rays of sunset. A bruise darkened the right side of his face.

"You heard?" he asked, voice rough as gravel.

Faith tied off her reins and climbed the steps, footsteps loud against the wood. "Donovan told me about Travis. About the ambush."

Nate shifted, wincing as he pushed himself upright, fingering the bruise. "We were close. Thought we had Pike's gang boxed in, that we might be able to get in and out before Pike caught wind... but he was waiting—like he knew we were coming."

Faith's stomach turned as she leaned against the porch rail, arms crossed tight. A chill breeze tugged at her sleeves, but she barely noticed.

Nate stared out at the horizon like it might offer answers, but Faith had questions of her own.

"Why did you trust Pierce?" she asked quietly. "Maybe he tipped Pike off."

"I don't see how he could've. Until I showed up, he didn't even know Travis was missing." Nate avoided her eyes. "Guess I trusted him because I had to."

"That's not an answer."

He sighed, jaw tightening. "Sterling came to me in town the other night. Said he wanted out, that he'd help us capture Pike, if I helped him."

Faith shook her head. "And you believed him? What if he's using you?"

"You think I didn't wonder too? But when it came down to it, he didn't run. He dragged Royce out under fire today. He got me back here alive. If he was still working with Pike, he would've shot us both and left our corpses to rot."

Faith studied him, arms folded across the chest of blue calico. "So, you trust him now because he helped you?"

"He didn't have to help. And honestly, I think he's sincere." Nate shifted, boots sliding against the porch boards. The rocking chair squeaked, *weeek, weeek*.

She let that settle in her mind, watching dust swirl around the yard. The porch's tin roof rattled above them. A couple chickens came squawking around the side of the house, pecking furiously at the ground, feathers puffed from the evening chill, wattles swaying.

"Where are Jed and Deck?" she asked, noticing how quiet it seemed.

"I sent 'em into town to stay with Royce," Nate said, rubbing the back of his neck. "June can nurse Royce's wound, and Jed won't realize I sent him for Royce to protect.. Truth is, I'm worried about him being here alone, even with Deck. I'm tired of surprises."

"I don't want another surprise, either." Her fingers tightened around the porch rail. "Not with Travis missing. Not with Pike and Hart circling like vultures."

Nate nodded slowly, studying the horizon. "Neither do I, and if we start doubting everyone, we'll be standin' alone when the next bullet flies."

"Then let's make sure we aim it the right way." She looked out at the gloaming, trying to steady her breath. "We can't afford to make another mistake. We need a plan."

"I've been thinkin'. Piecing it together." Nate eased from the rocker and stepped toward her. "Pike's got half the town scared stiff, and the other half's on Hart's payroll. But we've got some proof to show Talbot now. I found Jenkins's wagon, burnt out, in a ravine not far from here. He didn't just leave town."

Faith's breath caught. "Wait, wait... Donovan said Jenkins packed up and went east." She pressed a hand to her mouth, stepping back as if the porch itself had shifted beneath her. "To keep from paying taxes."

Nate's jaw clenched. "That's because no one was supposed to know. But I found Jenkins's burnt ledger—it's proof they didn't get far. The Jenkins family died right there in that wagon. Murdered."

Faith stared at him, horrified. "If Jenkins didn't leave, and someone covered it up... Are we already too late to stop this?"

"I'll never believe that," Nate answered, voice sharp with conviction. "We've got proof Jenkins and his family were murdered. Travis is missing. I might be able to get Pierce to tell the sheriff what he knows."

She stood abruptly, pacing the porch in tight, restless strides. The sound of her shoes echoed the tension in her chest. "Talbot can't ignore this, can he? Not with everything we've got."

Nate's laugh was bitter, low. "Talbot's scared—but maybe if we push hard enough, he'll have to listen." He stepped to the edge of the porch. "Travis and I found a stash of guns hidden in an old cabin. Sterling told us where to look, which is another reason I trust him. We destroyed them."

Faith's breath hitched. "You didn't tell me that."

"I didn't want to, not until I thought I could do something about it. Now, I'm thinking that's why they took him." Nate nodded grimly. "I wish we'd kept some rifles to show Talbot, but even without them, we have Jenkins's ledger. The papers Hart's lawyer gave you."

Faith looked at him questioningly.

"I went through them," Nate explained. "Half of 'em are forged, and the other half's bait. Hart's trying to bleed this town dry by buying up land cheap, then selling to the railroad for top dollar. It doesn't prove Pike is involved, but it might be enough."

Faith turned away, swallowing hard. Her eyes drifted toward the blackened shell of Nate's barn. "Not sure there's much to show, but those men ransacked my storeroom and beat up Donovan. Torched your barn. And you know about Pike paying me a visit."

She'd sent Donovan over to inform Nate that same night, but there hadn't been anything Nate could do, not with Pike gone.

He nodded. "Let me saddle Henry."

**

Niobrara

By the time they rode into town, the sky was bruised with deep purple. Lamp light shone from the jail, spilling across the wooden boardwalk.

Talbot sat behind his desk, arms crossed and jaw clenched, as they took turns telling him everything, spreading the evidence over his desk: Jenkins's blackened ledger, the papers from Hart's lawyer. Faith tried to stay hopeful, but one look at the sheriff's face made her heart sink to the toes of her high-buttoned shoes.

"I'm sorry," he said, voice clipped like he wasn't sorry at all, "but without witnesses or direct evidence, I can't pin anything on Pike or Hart. You say there were attacks, but no one actually saw who burnt your barn. No one saw who came after your ranch."

"You think Nate set his own barn on fire? You think I cut my own fences, lost my prized bull, and got Jackson knifed and nearly killed?" Faith stepped forward, her voice raising in both pitch and volume. She clenched the folds of her skirt, wishing she could grab the man and shake sense into him. "We *did* see the men who attacked Donovan."

"Wore masks, he said." Talbot didn't flinch, but he didn't meet her eyes either. "I think you're scared, and you're right to be. But scared don't equal proof."

"What about this?" Nate snatched up Jenkins's ledger and dropped it back on the desk with a *thud*. "I found what's left of the Jenkins family in the ravine south of my ranch, murdered and burned out. You can go out there and see. Jenkins didn't leave town—he was silenced by someone who wanted his land. Know anybody who fits that description, Sheriff?"

Talbot glanced at the book, but didn't touch it. "That's circumstantial. Anybody could have killed the Jenkinses."

Faith's voice cracked. "So is Travis disappearing after helping Nate destroy Hart's hidden gun stash. So are the forged papers Hart's lawyer gave me. So are the fires at my ranch and Nate's. How many 'coincidences' do you need before you admit what's under your own nose? How much proof do you need?"

The sheriff sighed ponderously, as if burdened by the fate of the entire world. "You didn't see him do it. Any of it."

"What?" Faith blinked, her voice tight with disbelief.

Talbot leaned forward, elbows on the desk, rubbing his temples with both hands. "You're saying Pike's responsible. Or Hart. But unless someone saw 'em personally committing a crime, I can't act. Not officially."

The room suddenly felt smaller, the lumber walls far too close. Nate stalked forward, the floorboards groaning beneath his determined stride.

"I need something I can take to the judge," Talbot continued, voice fraying at the edges. "A witness. A confession. Not a lot of 'maybes.'"

Nate's jaw tightened as he leaned in. "We're working on that. Pierce knows something more. He's scared, but he'll talk."

Talbot looked up, finally meeting Nate's gaze with bloodshot, doubt-rimmed eyes. "Then get him to talk. Because until someone does, Pike and Hart are just two men with money and influence, and I've got nothing but suspicions."

Faith's hands trembled at her sides, fists clenched to keep them steady. Her breath came shallow, her heart thudding against her ribs. She stepped forward, eyes locked on Talbot's. "Then we'll bring you more proof."

Talbot's eyes darted toward the window, then back to the floor. His voice lowered to a whisper. "You don't understand—they've got eyes everywhere. If I talk, I'm dead. My family, too."

Faith saw it clearly now: his hunched shoulders, the tremble in his hands—he wasn't just reluctant; he was *terrified*.

"Sheriff," she said gently, "we're not asking you to stand alone. We're asking you to help us stop this before it gets worse. Before anyone else gets hurt."

But Nate had already stepped forward, fists clenched; he looked ready to explode. "You think you're the only one with something to lose? Travis is missing. My barn's gone. Faith's suffered losses, and her hired hand got stabbed. Titus Jenkins and his family are dead. And you're worried about *yourself*?"

He slammed his fist on Talbot's desk, making the sheriff jump.

"You knew what that badge meant when you took this job. It comes with risks. Pike is an escaped prisoner! A wanted man!" Nate's voice cracked like a whip.

Talbot flinched, staring toward the door.

"You want to wait until Pike comes for you? Until Hart buys your land out from under you and buries your family in a shallow grave?"

"Nate!" Faith grabbed his arm, pulling him back. His breath was ragged, chest heaving with fury. "Stop—it's no use."

"You're right." He looked at her, eyes blazing, then turned away, growling like a caged animal. "We're wasting time here. He's not going to be any help."

Faith turned back to Talbot, voice soft but steady. "We understand that you're scared. So are we. But if we don't act now, we lose everything. Travis. The town. Maybe our lives."

Talbot stared at the floor, tight-lipped.

Faith stepped beside Nate, her hand still on his arm. "We're alone in this," she said quietly. "If we want to save Travis and stop Pike and Hart, it's just us."

The silence that followed was thick with the sheriff's fear.

Faith nudged Nate toward the door, using every bit of strength she had to keep him from lunging at Talbot.

Chapter Twenty-Three

Outlaw Camp

The cabin was quiet, except for the low hiss of the lantern and the occasional groan of the wind. Owen Pike stood at the center of the room, coat slung over the back of a chair, sleeves rolled to the elbow. His knuckles were still bruised from the last message he'd sent, one Travis Rivers hadn't been awake to receive.

Everett Pierce and Amos Parsons stood across from him, stiff-backed and silent. The fire between them crackled, but it didn't warm the room. Not with chilly gusts sneaking through holes in the chinking.

It's all Holt's fault we had to leave the better hideaway in the canyon—his, and Sterling Pierce's, the traitor.

"You did good with the deputy, Amos," Owen said, voice smooth as oil. "Quick. Quiet. No fuss. He got what he deserved, tailing us and trying to capture me again. Barett Rivers should have known better than to try to take up where he left off seventeen years ago."

Amos nodded once, his eyes flicking toward Everett, who hadn't moved.

"But Rivers was just a minor irritation," Owen continued, pacing slowly. "A pebble in the boot. Holt's the one who matters. He's the reason I spent seventeen years rotting in that cell."

He stopped and faced his men, eyes gleaming in the firelight.

"You know what it's like to be forgotten?" he demanded sharply. "To sit in a box while the world moves on, while the man who put you there walks free, builds a life, and kisses his wife, breathing clean air every morning?"

Everett swallowed hard. "Figure it's hard."

Owen nodded, smiling bitterly. "'Hard' don't cover it. Holt didn't just lock me up—he made me disappear, like I was nothing. Like I didn't matter. Me, Owen Pike, leader of the Coyote Clan."

He stepped closer, scuffing along the floor. "And now he's back, playing lawman, pretending he's got justice on his side. But justice ain't blind. It's *bought*—and Holt paid for it with my life."

Owen let the silence stretch, let the weight settle.

"And while Holt plays lawman," he said, voice tightening, "Sterling's been meeting with him behind our backs. You saw him the other day at the canyon, shooting at us. What do you have to say about that, Everett?"

Everett's jaw clenched. "He's my brother."

"And he betrayed you," Owen snapped. "Betrayed all of us."

Amos shifted uneasily, but the half-breed kept quiet.

He knows his place.

Owen didn't look away from Everett. "I warned you," he growled. "I don't tolerate betrayal. Not even from blood."

"I understand." Everett's eyes dropped to the floor.

"Do you?" Owen stepped so close he could smell the whiskey on Everett's breath. "Because you know what comes next. Sterling needs to pay for his treachery."

Everett looked up. "What do you want me to do?"

"I want you to be the one to punish him." Owen grinned. "Show the Coyotes what loyalty looks like. Let 'em see what happens when someone sides with the man who buried me alive."

Everett's face went pale. After a moment, he nodded stiffly. "He deserves it, I guess. If he talks, it could put a noose around all our necks. I ain't about to let anybody do that—not even my kid brother."

Owen clapped him on the shoulder. "You're learning, Pierce." He turned away, walking toward the back room. "Before we deal with Sterling, though, we must finish what we started. Our first business is with Nate Holt."

Amos nodded, but Everett hesitated. "You said you wanted him to suffer."

"And he will," Owen said, voice like a blade dragged slow across stone, "but first, we play with him a little, like a cat with a mouse."

The fire popped, sending a spray of sparks up the chimney. Shadows danced across the cracked walls of the cabin as Owen stood near the door to the back room, his eyes cast in shadow.

"We hit Holt where it hurts most: Jed, his son. Pretty li'l Miz Faith Shaw." He paused, savoring the name. "She's more than just a thorn in my side. She's fire. And I know how to douse a fire."

He laughed, a low, rasping sound. He'd been too long without a spirited woman in his arms.

Everett shifted again, boots scraping the floor.

"Don't worry," Owen teased. "I'll be gentle—at first. You want to know what suffering looks like? It's watching the people you love scream, knowing you can't stop it. Knowing the man who did it is still out there, still breathing, still smiling."

Everett's throat worked. "You mean to kill her?"

Owen's smile widened. "Eventually... but not before she sees the monster Nate Holt created. She'll beg before the end. Not for her life—she's too proud for that—no, she'll beg for *Holt's*."

Amos's eyes glinted as he fingered the knife in his scabbard.

"We're not just going to kill him," Owen continued. "We'll unravel him, piece by piece. First, his dear departed deputy's son. Then, the boy. Then, Faith and everything he's built."

He stopped, staring into the fire. "I want him to feel the same pain he made me feel, to wake up every morning wondering who's next. I want him to see the people he loves die, one by one, and know it's because of me."

He walked to the back of the cabin, boots thumping across the warped floorboards. The door to the back room creaked open. Lantern light spilled across the floor, revealing the slumped figure of Travis Rivers tied to a chair, head lolling forward. Blood streaked his shirt, both dried and fresh. One eye was swollen shut, the other barely open, glazed with pain.

Owen stepped inside and crouched beside the chair, fingers brushing Travis's chin. "Time to make you useful, boy."

Travis didn't stir.

"You're going to help us draw Holt out. You're going to be bait." Owen gripped the boy's chin hard with his hand.

Travis groaned faintly, eyelid fluttering.

Owen dropped the boy's face and walked back to the others. Outside, the wind had picked up, rattling the shutters as though clawing to get in.

"We'll head out at dawn," he declared. "Amos, get the horses ready. Everett, go find your brother. Take care of him so he can't tattle to Holt."

Everett hesitated. "And if he runs?"

Owen's grin widened as he held out his hands to the warmth. "Then you chase him—and don't stop until he's on his knees with a bullet in his brain."

Chapter Twenty-Four

The floorboards creaked beneath Nate as he shifted, an old quilt tangled around his legs. Sleeping on a pallet reminded him of old times. Many a night, he and Barrett had settled on the floor in a stranger's parlor while trailing an outlaw.

Jed breathed steadily beside him, a soft rhythm in the dark. Outside, a restless breeze whispered through the cottonwoods. The ranch had settled into uneasy silence, too quiet for comfort, too still for peace.

Faith slept in Nate's room—or, more likely, *tried* to sleep, like he'd been doing. Nate doubted she'd closed her eyes. After they'd left that poor excuse of a sheriff, Nate had picked up Jed and Deck. June decided to stay in town with Lydia Burke.

"I'll be praying for you to find Travis," she'd said, "but I'll feel safer behind brick walls and a locked door."

Nate couldn't blame her. He hadn't exactly planned on asking Faith to come, but the invitation had just slipped out.

He'd half expected her to decline his offer—she was proud, independent, and had every reason to keep her distance—but she'd surprised him by agreeing with a quiet nod and a knowing look in her eyes, as though she'd guessed what he'd left unsaid.

Truthfully, it felt nice to have a woman bustling around the kitchen again. Nate certainly hadn't minded getting a mouthwatering meal in the bargain. He could still taste her savory stew, and those featherlight biscuits—golden on the outside, soft as clouds inside—had almost made him forget the world was falling apart.

The biscuits had come out of the oven steaming, brushed with butter, and sprinkled with salt. He'd taken one bite and closed his eyes. They tasted so good, his shoulders had dropped, the tension in his jaw easing for the first time in days. He'd eaten three before realizing he was full, then reached for a fourth anyway.

For a few hours, the ranch had felt like something out of a memory, like the happy years with Etta, before resentment and fear had turned her against him.

Faith had moved through the kitchen confidently, sleeves rolled up, hair tied back, humming quietly as she worked. Jed had set the table without being asked while Deck curled up on the porch in quiet contentment, gnawing on a stew bone. Faith had served stew with a ladle that clinked against the enamel pot, and when she passed Nate his bowl, their fingers had brushed for just enough for him to notice how soft they felt. The brief contact had shot an unexpected thrill straight through him.

They'd lingered at the table longer than usual. Jed had asked Faith about when she was a little girl.

Faith had laughed. "I was a naughty little girl. Mama was a schoolteacher in Bellevue, and she used to say I spent more time standing in the corner than the rest of the children combined."

Jed had giggled like the kid he was, and a smile had tugged Nate's lips as Faith related some of her misdeeds.

It had been easy to pretend the world outside didn't exist, to forget about the fire in the barn, the threats that brooded over them like storm clouds. Owen Pike had felt miles away. The ranch had felt safe. Happy.

Nate had caught himself watching Faith as she cleared the dishes, the way her eyes had softened when Jed asked more questions.

He'd asked her to come for her protection, but truth was, he'd wanted her there. Wanted her voice in the house, wanted her to see the life he'd built since hanging up his guns.

And for a few golden hours, she had.

Now, lying on the floor with Jed asleep beside him, Nate stared at the ceiling and tried to hold onto that feeling. The warmth. The laughter. The taste of stew and biscuits and something like hope.

Suddenly, a loud *crack* split the night, like lightning striking dry timber.

Nate bolted upright.

I knew it couldn't last.

Chapter Twenty-Five

Jed jumped up, eyes wide in a pale face. "Pa? What's wrong?"

Deck gave one short bark and growled low in his throat, the hair bristling on the back of his scruffy neck.

"Quiet, Deck!" Already moving, Nate shoved back the kitchen table and lifted the trap door. "Get in the cellar, Jed, and stay there."

Jed scrambled toward the opening and hurried down the ladder, chirping for Deck to follow. Nate helped them down into the dark, then slid the trap door back into place. Dust puffed up around his knees as he dropped the rag rug back over the door.

Another shot echoed, closer this time; then, a brilliant light shone through the window, followed by the unmistakable roar of fire.

"Sounds like we got visitors," Faith called as she hurried into the main room. Although her green dress looked wrinkled, she'd bound her hair in a neat braid, and she gripped a revolver. She didn't hesitate or ask questions.

She was ready to help him defend the ranch.

Nate grabbed his rifle from the mantel above the fireplace. "Stay low."

He cracked the front door and peered out. Smoke rolled across the yard in thick, choking waves. An orange glow engulfed the shed, flames licking up its sides and casting jagged shadows across the ground. The chicken coop was already gone, just a pile of embers and scorched wire. The lean-to behind it crackled violently, its roof sagging as fire chewed through the beams.

Thankfully, the chickens had escaped to run around the barnyard, shrieking but unharmed. Henry and Faith's mare, Delilah, galloped away from the flames, eyes rolling.

"Come on," Nate said, pushing the door open wider. He stepped onto the porch. Faith followed, crouched low, as a wave of blistering heat hit them, accompanied by the stink of ash and burning hay.

There goes my winter feed.

The panicked cattle were screaming; they crashed against the corral fence until it gave way with an abrupt, splintering *crack*.

A stampede burst through the pasture, hooves pounding, horns flashing. The ground trembled beneath them.

Nate shoved Faith behind him as a wild-eyed steer barreled past, foam streaking its muzzle. Its broad side clipped the porch rail, sending splinters flying.

"Durn it," Nate muttered. "That's the third time I've fixed that fence."

Figures moved through the smoke: men on horseback, faces masked. At least six riders, maybe more. They rode in from the east, silhouettes flickering in the firelight, weaving between the stampeding cattle like phantoms.

The new Coyote Clan?

Nate raised his rifle and fired. One rider pitched sideways as his horse reared in panic and bolted into the smoke. Not waiting to discover the man's fate, Nate turned, searching for the next threat.

Faith fired next, steady despite the chaos. Her bullet clipped another rider's shoulder, spinning him off his mount. With a grunt, he hit the ground and rolled, disappearing behind a hay bale as his horse fled, reins trailing.

The outlaws moved fast, circling like vultures, their horses kicking up dirt. Muzzle flashes lit the smoke as they fired at the house, into the trees, toward anything that moved. Bullets shattered windows of the cabin, punched through porch posts, tore through the walls. A lantern inside shattered, spilling pungent kerosene.

Nate ducked as a round whizzed past his ear, close enough to feel the heat. A beat later, red-hot pain sliced through his arm like a knife. He staggered, nearly dropping his rifle, and caught himself on the porch rail, blood soaking through his sleeve.

"You're hit!" Faith shouted, ducking behind the rocking chair as another bullet punched through the log wall inches from her head, wood chips raining down.

"Hit, but not down," Nate ground out through clenched teeth. He dropped to one knee and fired again, this time aiming for a rider weaving between the cattle and catching him in the thigh. The outlaw screamed and toppled sideways, his horse crashing into the fence. A second later, he was back on his feet, limping after his horse.

Faith rolled out from cover and fired twice in quick succession. One bullet struck a rider's rifle, knocking it from his hands; the second hit his saddle, sending the horse bucking and snorting into the chaos.

Nate gritted his teeth, chambered another round, and fired at a rider flanking left. The man ducked, but the bullet clipped his boot, sending his horse through the garden fence, trampling rows of beans and squash.

Smoke thickened, choking the air. Sparks drifted like fireflies across the yard, raining soot and ash. A heavy smell of burning kerosene and scorched hay filled the air.

"We've got to move," Nate rasped. "They'll torch everything, and Jed's still in the house."

Faith's eyes were locked on the shed, a small but deadly inferno. Flames leapt toward the eaves of the house, smoke curling into the sky.

"We can't hold them off," she said finally, "and if an ember hits the house..."

"I'm sorry," Nate mumbled, a hand to the wound on his shoulder. Blood seeped through his fingers as his arm grew numb, his grip weakening. He could barely keep the rifle steady.

I couldn't keep them safe. It was his worst nightmare. He could only repeat to Faith, "I'm sorry," until a new sound came through the night.

Slow, deliberate hoofbeats—not the frantic rhythm of attack, but calmer, steadier.

Nate turned toward the sound, and the world seemed to tip on its axis.

Owen Pike emerged from the smoke like a specter of the past, straight-backed as a king in the saddle. His horse moved with eerie calm, seemingly unbothered by the madness of squawking chickens and crazed cattle. Firelight danced across Pike's face, his eyes gleaming in devilish delight beneath the brim of his hat.

Behind him, tied by the wrists and dragged through the dirt, was Travis.

The youth's head lolled, face swollen and bloodied, mouth slack. His shirt was soaked through, streaked with blood and soot. Every few feet, his body jerked as the rope tied to Pike's saddle pulled taut.

Nate froze. His breath caught. His knees buckled. The rifle slipped from his hands and clattered to the porch floor.

He couldn't move.

Couldn't speak.

Pike reined in just beyond the burning shed, his horse standing still as flames crackled around him. He looked older, leaner, the years carved into his skin like dry riverbeds, but his eyes were unchanged. Cold. Calculating. Full of hate.

He looked like a demon from hell as he stared straight at Nate and smiled.

Not a grin. Not a sneer. Just a quiet, knowing smirk.

Like he'd already won.

Nate's vision blurred. His chest felt hollow, like his heart had been scooped out. The fight drained from him all at once, leaving only the weight of failure, thick and suffocating.

Maybe Etta was right.

The porch felt cold beneath his knees. He could hear the inferno chewing through the shed, the brittle snap of timber, the low groan of collapsing beams. Deck's frantic barking from the root cellar. Faith's ragged breathing. But it all sounded distant, like it belonged to someone else's nightmare.

The bitter taste of defeat rose in his throat.

We're going to die.

And Owen Pike had come to watch it happen, like a man admiring the last light of a sunset he'd painted himself.

"Well," Pike drawled. "Ain't this a treat, us meeting again like this, Sheriff Holt? Been a long time—seventeen years, as I recall. Last time I saw you was at my trial, the day before they locked me in a cell. But I ain't never forgot you, Holt."

Refusing to give up, Nate forced himself to his feet. He managed to lift the rifle, though his arms trembled. "Let Travis go. If you want revenge, we'll settle it between the two of us. Let Faith and the boy go. When they walk away free, I'll be your prisoner."

Pike's bitter laugh echoed through the night. "You're in no position to bargain, Holt."

The remaining Coyotes rode up behind him like wolves waiting for the signal to tear into flesh.

"You want the Rivers boy back?" Pike said, tilting his head. "Then Miz Shaw there sells her ranch. She packs up and leaves and never comes back. And you, Holt, you just turn the other way an' forget this little visit here."

Faith stepped beside Nate, revolver steady. "You're insane."

"No." Pike's smile widened. "I'm *patient*. You've got until sundown two days from now. After that..." He glanced over his shoulder at Travis, bound and bloodied at the end of the rope, then back at Nate. "He dies—slow—and then, I'll come back for you."

Nate's grip tightened on the rifle, knuckles white. "You better not touch him, Pike, or so help me, I'll track you down and—"

Pike leaned forward in the saddle with a wicked wink. "I already have."

One of the outlaws snickered.

Nate's breath caught in fear. Rage surged, hot and blinding, as he saw the bruises on Travis's face, the shallow rise and fall of his chest. It looked like Travis had been beaten within an inch of his life.

Pike wasn't bluffing. In that moment, Nate knew surrender wasn't an option. Pike wouldn't stop with Faith's ranch; he'd take more and more, not stopping until he owned everything, leaving corpses in his wake.

Despite the anger burning in Nate's chest, he forced himself to stay calm. This wasn't about land; it was about power. Pike resented those years in prison, and now, he planned to watch Nate lose everything.

Nate lowered the rifle just enough to steady his aim. His voice came low, steady, and firm. "Then you'd better kill me now, Pike, because I won't let you win. Faith ain't selling her ranch, and if you kill Travis, I'll see you hang this time."

Pike's smile faltered—just a flicker, but enough for Nate to see that he'd rattled the man.

Faith didn't move, but Nate felt her small, warm hand squeeze his arm.

The Coyotes stirred uncertainly, and for the first time since Pike had appeared, Nate felt solid ground beneath him again.

I'm not done yet.

Then, with a cruel laugh, Pike turned and rode off into the smoke, dragging Travis behind him. It took every ounce of control Nate had to restrain himself from putting a bullet in Pike's back.

Almost as though she'd sensed his thoughts, Faith gripped his arm firmly and whispered, "He's not worth it."

The Coyote Clan disappeared into the night like shadows as the blackened skeletons of the shed and lean-to collapsed, showering the smoldering air with luminous particles.

From inside the cabin, Nate heard Deck's muffled barking. His shoulder screamed in pain as he surveyed the destruction. Exhausted cattle ranged all over the barnyard and pastures. Chickens ran here and there, searching for their missing coop. It would take hours to round all the animals up, repair the fence and coop.

Two days. That didn't give them much time to come up with a plan.

Chapter Twenty-Six

Smoke hung low over the yard, crawling aimlessly through broken fence posts and scorched grass. Faith shut the door on the destruction as the pinkish wash of sunrise rose in the east.

It had taken a while to persuade Nate to stop pacing the yard as though he could will the damage away. He'd already tried hauling off a half-burned beam with one arm, teeth gritted, blood dripping down to his wrist. Faith had caught up to him at the edge of the yard.

"Nate, stop. You're bleeding."

"I've got work to do."

"You've got a hole in your arm," she'd retorted, stepping in front of him, "and you can't fix *anything* if you're passed out in the dirt. Besides, Jed and Deck are still in the cellar, probably frightened half to death."

He'd looked past her, toward the shed, where the flames had finally died, his eyes distant, unfocused. "I can't even feel the pain, but... I reckon you're right. Jed's probably scared."

Even so, Faith had to force Nate to move, his feet dragging as she gripped his good arm and tugged him across the yard. The front door groaned as she pushed it open, smoke trailing in behind them.

Inside, the cool air reeked of scorched wood and spilled kerosene. She crossed to the trapdoor beneath the table, pulled off the rug, and knocked twice.

A moment later, Jed called up, his voice shaky but eager. "Pa?"

"We're here," Faith said gently. "It's safe. Come on out."

The trap door flipped open. Jed's head appeared after a moment, wide eyes searching Faith's face as she smiled, doing her best to project calm.

Jed climbed up, then lifted Deck out. Blinking against the light, Jed rushed to Nate's side while Deck gave a half-hearted bark and nosed around the floor.

Faith guided Nate to the kitchen and sat him firmly in a chair. "Jed, could you fetch some water, please? And find some spare cloth to tear into bandages."

Nate mumbled something about rags in a chest under the bed.

"Is he shot?" Jed's voice rose in fear at the sight of so much blood.

"Just a flesh wound," Faith replied with practiced brightness, just as Mama had done when she didn't want Faith to worry. "Get the water so I can clean your pa up."

The boy hurried to obey, bringing a basin of water and a bundle of old, ripped shirts. Water sloshed over his hands in his eagerness to help.

Faith knelt beside Nate, carefully tearing his bloody sleeve away from his shoulder. She probed gently at the wound, but he still flinched. "You should have this stitched up."

Nate shook his head. His face was pale beneath the smudges of soot, his jaw clenched beneath the beard like he was holding back more than pain. "It's nothing."

"It's *not* nothing."

Faith swallowed hard. She wanted to shake him, to make him see that he wasn't invincible. But she knew better; like her Caleb, Nate Holt wouldn't bend until he broke.

She pressed a clean strip of cloth to the gash on his arm. Blood soaked through the bandage quickly, but he didn't pull away.

Jed hovered nearby, arms crossed, plainly trying to look tough. All the same, his moist eyes betrayed his distress, flicking from the blood on Nate's arm to his face.

"I want to help," he said suddenly, voice cracking. "I can fight."

Nate's head whipped around. "Don't be ridiculous," he snapped. "This is my battle—*mine*. Not yours."

"I'm not a kid anymore!"

"You're twelve," Nate argued, but beneath his anger, Faith heard a mixture of pride and disbelief that the boy was standing there, trying to be a man.

Jed's mouth tightened. "I'm not scared."

"Well, you should be," Nate said, softer now. He reached out and gripped Jed's shoulder. "You're brave, son, but you don't have to fight." He grinned. "Not yet, anyway. We got lots of years before you do."

Jed blinked hard, nodding once, but his lip trembled.

Nate pulled him into a quick, fierce hug, then let go just as fast.

Faith's heart ached. Here, Nate was—worn down, bleeding, and half broken, yet ready to take a bullet to keep his son from harm. That kind of love didn't come easily or often.

She tied off the bandage and sat back on her heels. "I've done the best I can. You'd do better to have Doc look at it."

"I've survived worse." Nate reached out and ruffled Jed's hair, then stood slowly, flinching as he tested the arm. "Jed, guess we'd best go out and see if we can put together another chicken coop, fix the fence, and round up the cattle. After I find a clean shirt."

"I'll start breakfast," Faith said, shaking her head.

Stubborn man.

A short time later, as Faith turned fried potatoes in the cast iron skillet, the urgent rhythm of hooves shattered the morning. She froze, fear seizing her heart. It couldn't be Nate and Jed; they'd walked toward the creek with rope, hoping to lead some cows home while she cooked.

She grabbed her revolver from the counter and hurried to the porch. Her breath caught as she searched the tree line, half expecting Pike to come riding back for more.

When she saw the riders, however, she relaxed her grip on the gun. Three horses cut through the yard, familiar silhouettes against the morning sky: Donovan, Lydia, and Sterling Pierce, faces drawn as they took in the smoldering destruction.

"We saw smoke from the ridge," Donovan called as he swung down from his horse. "What happened? Is everyone all right?"

Faith exhaled, her throat dry. The tension beneath her bodice eased enough to speak. "Owen Pike happened."

Pierce dismounted and stomped over the charred grass. His eyes swept the yard, lingering on the blackened fence, smoking remains of the shed and coop, and crimson stain on the porch.

"Where's Nate?"

Faith stared at the wreckage, the smoke curling around smoldering piles of charred wood. "He went to—" she began, then stopped short as Nate strode across the yard, his bandaged arm stiff at his side.

"What happened here, Nate?" Donovan asked. "Did you get hit?"

Nate glanced at the bandage, then muttered, "It's nothing. Pike came mostly to leave a message."

Pierce's eyes darted back and forth, as though expecting an ambush. "What kind of message?"

"He wants Faith's ranch. He had Travis with him," Nate replied. "He said if we don't give him what he wants by sundown tomorrow, Travis dies."

Faith clamped her trembling hands into fists, feeling the weight of responsibility squeeze her chest. Travis's life was in her hands; if she refused to sell...

Does my ranch really matter when a young man's life is hanging in the balance?

"Pike wants blood, and he's not working alone." Lydia's voice simmered with resentment as she dismounted in one smooth motion. "Hart's behind this—I'd bet my saddle on it. They've already run me out of business. Don't you dare sell them your ranch, Faith."

Faith's gaze roved over the scorched earth, the buildings that would take weeks to rebuild. Jed was scared. Nate had been shot. Travis might not live until sundown.

And her home, the last piece of Caleb's legacy, was the reason for all the trouble.

What would Caleb do?

"We can't do this alone," Faith said finally, her voice tight as she looked around at her friends. "We're outnumbered.

Outgunned. I don't know if we can stop Pike, and I don't know if we should even try. Is my ranch even worth it?"

Pierce spoke up, his voice firm. "You've got something they want. That means you've got power. If we stand together, they won't get to take it without a fight."

Donovan stepped closer, reaching out to grasp Faith's hand. "You're not alone."

Faith looked up, startled by the steadiness in his voice, his reassuring squeeze, and Lydia's encouraging smile.

"I've been talking to folks," Donovan said. "Quiet-like. Ranchers who've lost stock. Families who've been threatened. People are sick of Hart and Pike running this valley like it's theirs."

Faith blinked. Words failed her. Since all this began, one of her biggest fears had been that Donovan would leave. He'd been beaten, Lydia's store ransacked, yet he hadn't run away. Sudden tears stung her eyes at the depth of the Burkes' friendship.

"I been out to gather support," Donovan said. "People are scared, but they're angry too. If we stand together…"

"We might have a chance," Nate finished for him. "Let's go inside and figure out a plan over breakfast."

Faith felt a crack form in the wall she'd built around herself after Caleb's death. She hadn't let herself believe she could hold out against Hart. Not really. Not alone. Now, there was danger from someone else—Owen Pike and his gang.

But now, she saw a small spark of hope.

"I sure hope those potatoes ain't burned to a crisp," Nate remarked teasingly. "They smell a mite done."

"The potatoes!" Faith hurried into the cabin, feeling lighter than she had since before Caleb died.

Chapter Twenty-Seven

They moved inside, gathering around the kitchen table, while Lydia helped Faith finish cooking a hearty breakfast. The comforting smells helped settle everyone's nerves, at least a little.

Sterling scribbled notes between bites, his brow furrowed in concentration as Lydia listed supplies they could scrounge from leftover stock at the store.

"We should find ammunition, lantern oil, spare tack..." she said as she walked around the table, pouring coffee. "I'll have to see what else. Might as well use what we have to fight Pike."

Donovan spread out a crude map of the town and outlying ranches drawn in charcoal on butcher paper. "We've got six confirmed people to help," he said, tapping the edge of the map. "I've talked to the McCall brothers, the Holloway twins, and Widow Nelson from Dry Creek. She's got a double-barrel and no patience left."

Lydia chuckled, placing the enamel coffeepot back on the stove and wiping her hands on a blue apron. "She's worth three men."

Sterling nodded. "I can get word to the Holloways. They've been itching for a reason to stand up to Pike. He wounded their uncle not long ago, and they know me." He gave everyone a sheepish grin. "They never rode with Pike, but their uncle did, so they've had dealings with him before."

"Wish we'd been here when Pike came calling." Donovan pushed aside the map to take a last bite of egg. "I'd have liked to see Travis for myself."

Nate stayed silent for most of it, arms crossed, eyes shadowed, but he winced when Donovan mentioned Travis. His fingers tapped the table when Sterling spoke of Pike's men.

He's as angry as the night we stormed out of Talbot's office and itching for a fight.

As Faith cleared the table, the small thread of hope she'd felt grew stronger. They were building something—a plan, a way to resist Pike's evil scheme—and for the first time in days, Faith felt like she could breathe.

***

The sun dipped low, casting long shadows across the yard. It had been a long, hardworking day. Throughout the day, the others had pitched in without hesitation to pull Nate's ranch back into order. Donovan helped Nate reinforce the porch, hammering in fresh planks where fire had chewed through the supports.

Sterling had spent hours checking the fencing, marking weak spots, and finding cattle along the back trail while Jed and Deck trailed happily behind. Even Lydia had insisted on helping, hauling buckets of water and mopping dirt and ash from the kitchen floor, washing dishes, tidying the house. Faith figured it might have been years since the windows were washed. Maybe as long ago as the day Nate's wife left.

By dusk, the ranch looked less like a ruin and more like a home again. The men had even ridden to Faith's and brought back a wagonload of spare lumber. With it, they rebuilt a rough outline of the barn and a small coop to house the chickens. The sound of hammering echoed through the afternoon, voices talking and laughing, though Travis was never out of mind.

As the sky purpled, Lydia pulled off an apron and hung it over the back of a chair. "Looks like that one has the right idea." She chuckled and nodded at Jed, who'd fallen asleep on the parlor floor with his boots still on. Deck lay wearily beside him, tongue lolling. When Lydia spoke, the dog thumped his tail.

"It's been a long day," Faith answered, weary beyond saying.

Sterling peeked into the cabin. "Lydia? Donovan has the horses saddled. He said he's ready when you are."

"I'm coming."

"I told Nate we'll circle the ridge and check the creek trail," Sterling told Faith. "If Pike's Coyotes are sniffing around, we'll spot 'em before they get close."

Faith followed them onto the porch, wrapping a blue shawl around her shoulders against the chill. "Be careful."

"We always are." Lydia gave a half-smile. "See you tomorrow."

Sterling swung into the saddle. "You've got a darned good reason to fight, and we're going to help."

Donovan lingered, then turned to Faith, touching her shoulder with a brotherly pat. "I meant what I said. I'm not leaving. Not now. Not ever."

Faith nodded as tears stung her eyes, barely whispering, "Thank you."

He smiled, then mounted up and waved as they left and rode toward town, hooves muffled on the hard-packed dirt. Across the barnyard, Faith saw a small glow of lantern light. Nate, checking the new fencing. The Burkes and Sterling reined in to speak to him for a few minutes, and Faith turned to go check on Jed.

A short time later, she found Nate on the porch, staring out at the dark. The sun had slid below the horizon, leaving dark slashes of shadow, making monsters of tree trunks and fence posts. The cool air was heavy with smoke, ash, and the scent of freshly sawed lumber. The silence felt too big for the night, broken only by faint rustling from the new chicken coop and the low murmur of insects.

The golden light of a lantern swinging from the porch rafter flickered across Nate's face, marking the weariness etched deep into the lines around his eyes. Somehow, he seemed older, like Pike's visit and fear for Travis had carved something out of him.

His eyes searched the horizon like he could bring Travis home with sheer force of will. He carried the weight of everyone's problems without complaint, not giving up, even as the Coyote Clan did its worst.

Faith reached out, brushing his bristly beard, wanting to offer comfort. Hope. Her fingers lightly traced his lips, feeling the firm, solid warmth of them and aching...

He didn't pull away.

I want to feel his lips on mine.

She stood beside him, heart pounding, unsure if it was the cold or the closeness that made her shiver. The porch felt like the edge of the world, and she didn't know if they'd still be alive tomorrow. But right now, at this moment, she needed something real. Something warm.

And yet, her thoughts darted to Caleb. His name rose like a flower pressed in a book, faded, withered, gone. The man she'd buried. The man she'd loved. She felt disloyal even thinking it, standing here with Nate's face beneath her fingers.

Caleb had been steady, kind, hers. But he was gone. And Nate was here—bruised, bleeding, and stubborn, but very much alive.

She didn't know what tomorrow would bring. But tonight, she wanted to feel something other than fear.

She looked down and leaned in. Her breath caught as she gave him time to pull away.

He didn't.

Their lips met, soft and tentative at first, then surer. Nate froze for half a breath, then kissed her back, his warm lips capturing hers. His hand found her cheek, rough and gentle all at once. She hadn't thought she could ever feel this way again. Not after all those lonely, fearful years without Caleb.

It wasn't planned. It wasn't perfect. But it was honest and deeply felt. The world didn't end as Faith had feared it might. Somehow, she even had a feeling Caleb might approve.

When they pulled apart, she rested her forehead against his. "We'll keep fighting," she whispered. "We'll bring Travis home and put Pike back behind bars."

Nate captured her fingers in one calloused hand and gave them a gentle kiss. "We'll sure enough try." Then, as if embarrassed, Nate jumped up. "Better check the livestock before bed. Goodnight."

"Goodnight, Nate," she whispered, but he was already lost in the gloaming.

Chapter Twenty-Eight

Nate made sure Faith spread the rumor the next morning, long before Pike's sundown deadline. She'd ridden into Niobrara at dawn to throw out the lies, while he stayed hidden nearby in case of trouble. *I'm ready to sell. Desperate, in fact, to save young Travis Rivers' life.*

"I told Maud at Wilson's Mercantile," Faith recounted after she'd returned to join Nate, "loud enough for a couple customers to overhear. I'm sure one of them works for Hart. Then, I went to the post office, the bank, and even Sheriff Talbot. I made sure to chatter to every gossip in town."

"What did you say?" Nate asked, helping her dismount from Delilah when they reached her ranch.

"That I'm tired of fighting. If Pike wants the land, he can have it. I'll sign at sundown." Faith grinned "I think I was convincing."

Word traveled fast, just as they'd hoped. Hart's men were greedy, predictable. When Hart's lawyer came riding over to sign papers, Faith told him, "I'll sign when Owen Pike returns Travis. Not a second before."

The man rode off in a huff.

Not that they planned to wait for sundown—Travis's life might depend on moving sooner.

As soon as Hart's lawyer left, Nate and Faith saddled up for the ride back to his ranch. The plan was to ambush Pike before he returned to Faith's ranch.

"Everyone ready to ride?" Nate asked as the group assembled in the barnyard, checking over supplies. "Royce wanted to come, but Doc says he needs more time to heal from our last run-in with the Coyotes. So, it's just us and the people you talked to, Donovan."

"Hope everything goes ok, Pa." Jed stood near Henry, stroking the gelding's nose. At his feet, Deck whimpered, as though knowing he'd be left behind with Lydia and Jed

"Keep the home fires burning." Nate smiled down at his son. "We'll be home soon." He forced himself to keep his back straight, to wave cheerfully as they rode away. In his heart, though, he knew the dangers only too well.

God, if you could, let me come home to my boy.

***

The hills were quiet, but not peaceful. It was the kind of quiet that came before a storm, when even the birds hold their breath.

Nate crouched behind a thicket of scrub oak, eyes locked on the trail below. His rifle rested across his knees, steady as his breath, though his heart beat like a drum in a funeral march. In the holster around his waist, his Colt was loaded and ready.

Despite his hopes Faith would choose to stay behind on the ranch, she crouched two yards to his left, revolver drawn. A strand of auburn hair clung to her cheek, damp with sweat. She hadn't spoken in ten minutes, her pale face set like carved stone.

Nate touched his lips, remembering the sweet taste of her lips the night before.

If we survive, maybe...

Donovan and Sterling spread out along the rim, buried in brush and shadow, but close enough for Nate to hear a quiet sneeze and a gulp. Sterling had a flask tucked under his coat. Donovan had a knife in his boot and a prayer on his lips.

A flicker of movement on the trail below. A cloud of dust. The steady *clip-clop* of hooves.

"They're here," Donovan whispered.

Nate raised the spyglass, narrowing his gaze on the distant trail. Pike rode at the front, unmistakable even from afar, his black hat pulled low. Behind him, a ragged line of riders followed, tense and watchful, dust rising in their wake.

"*'Will you walk into my parlour?' said the Spider to the Fly...*" Nate muttered.

To the east, tucked behind a fallen cottonwood, the Holloway twins lay prone in the leaf litter. When Nate had checked on them earlier, Caleb had a Remington cradled against his shoulder, his cheek pressed to the stock. His brother, Cash, had his sights set with a Spencer carbine, his breathing slow and deliberate.

Farther west, near an old mining shaft, the McCall brothers were ready and waiting.

And finally, tucked in the hollow of a dry creek bed, Widow Nelson waited with a shard of mirror and a pocketful of snuff. She had no weapon; her job wasn't to shoot, but to distract. At just the right moment, she'd catch sunlight with the mirror, blinding Pike's mount.

The snuff was for her comfort. "A last bit of life's temptation, iffen I should meet my maker today," she'd cackled.

Nate lowered the spyglass, clenching his teeth so tightly that his jaw ached. "Eight riders," he murmured. "Pike, two flankers, the rest behind."

He adjusted the lens, breath catching as he focused in on the last horse in line, a loose-limbed bay.

Travis slumped in the saddle like a rag doll, hands bound, face a mess of bruises and dried blood. But he was breathing.

Still alive.

Nate's breath came sharp, like he'd been punched. He lowered the glass and turned to Faith, voice shaking. "I'm going to rescue him."

Faith grabbed his arm. "No—not yet. Wait until they come closer!"

"I can't." His voice cracked. "Look at him."

"I see him," she replied, "but if you go now, you'll get yourself killed. Travis, too."

Nate shook her off, fury rising like bile. "They've got him roped like a steer. He's half-dead. You want me to sit here while Pike parades him through that canyon like a trophy?"

Faith stepped in front of him, blocking his path. "You think I don't care? You think I haven't been staring at that trail for two hours, praying he's still alive?"

Nate's fists clenched. "Then help me *do* something!"

"We are," she insisted firmly. "We boxed in the trail. Pike's leading them straight into it. The canyon narrows at the bend; there's brush on both sides, nowhere to run. Donovan and Sterling are set on the rim. As soon as Miz Nelson distracts Pike's horse, we can attack. One shot from Sterling, and we close the trap. Even if they ride toward the ranch, the Holloways and McCalls will stop them."

Nate's eyes flicked to the canyon mouth. The riders were nearing the opening. Travis's horse stumbled, and he swayed dangerously.

"I should've gone last night," Nate muttered.

"You'd be dead," Faith said flatly, "and Travis would still be in that saddle." Her voice softened. "Let the plan work. We've got it all figured out—Nate! No!"

He was already moving, low and fast, through the brush. Every step sent fire into his chest. He had one plan now: get behind the riders and save Travis. Nate slid down the rocky trail, careful to keep hidden from the men in the lead.

An owl's call trilled in the air. The signal. A second later, Pike's horse shied as a ray of sun flashed into his eyes.

Sterling's rifle cracked.

The shot had been meant for Pike, but it struck the canyon wall instead, sending a shower of rock chips down onto the riders. Horses reared. Shouts rang out. One of the outlaws fired blindly toward the ridge, and Donovan cursed, ducking behind a boulder.

The canyon erupted. Gunfire echoed off the stone, ricocheting in every direction. Pike's horse bolted sideways, nearly unseating him. Miz Nelson dove for cover as Pike wheeled his mount, eyes wild, and bellowed, "Head for the ranch!"

But the canyon bend was too narrow. Brush caught stirrups and reins. One outlaw was thrown as his horse tangled in a thicket. Another fired upward, forcing Sterling to retreat from the ridge.

Then, Travis's horse buckled again, legs trembling.

Nate scrambled up the slope and reached Travis just as he slid from the saddle, catching him before he hit the rocks.

"I've got you," Nate whispered, breath ragged, his arms sagging from the youth's weight. Thankfully, Pike and his men were too busy to concern themselves with what happened behind them.

Travis blinked, dazed. "Sheriff Nate?"

"Hold on."

On the trail in front of them, outlaws surged in every direction, some doubling back, others charging forward. A few broke through the trap, galloping toward the open plain.

A trio of riders veered west, toward Nate's ranch—Pike led the charge, shouting, blood streaked across his face. Everett and Amos flanked him, firing wildly behind them to slow pursuit.

Faith shouted up in the hills. Donovan fired again, but the canyon was choked with dust and confusion. Horses screamed. A second rifle cracked from the rim in the direction of Holloway's hiding place, but it was too late.

Pike was getting away.

At least I have Travis.

Nate pulled the youth into the brush, shielding him with his body as the canyon rang with gunshots. In the middle of it all, Nate had one chance to get them both out alive.

"Stay down," he told Travis. "I'll come back for you."

Weakly, Travis managed a nod and crawled into a small thicket of vines.

The fight had turned; gun smoke still hung in the air, but the Coyotes were breaking through, kicking up dirt and grit as they headed west. The others—probably Hart's men—had scattered or fallen, but those three were fast, desperate, and dangerous.

"They're heading for the ranch!" Faith shouted, reloading as she ran for the horses.

Nate didn't hesitate.

Jed!

Chapter Twenty-Nine

Nate vaulted toward the ridge, pounding up the trail. Donovan and Sterling followed, cutting through the creek bed to flank him. Caleb Holloway fired once more from the ridge, forcing Pike to duck low in the saddle.

But the outlaws didn't stop. They were headed straight for Nate's ranch, and he was going to stop them.

Lungs burning, Nate pulled himself on Henry's broad back and rode like a man possessed. The ranch was just over the rise. He could see the gate, the porch, the framework of the new barn, and the riders closing in.

This time, it would end.

I'm done running.

Gunfire cracked across the yard as he slid from the saddle and slapped Henry's rump to send him out of danger. Nate crouched behind the feed trough, his Colt gripped in his hand, slick with sweat. He darted a glance toward the cabin, but saw no sign of movement. Hopefully, Lydia had taken Jed and Deck into the root cellar when she'd heard gunfire.

Taking a chance, Nate ducked behind the lean-to. The acrid stench of black powder filled his nose, mingling with the sharp tang of scorched wood, though he saw no flames.

Sterling hollered from a nearby cottonwood tree as Donovan's revolver popped from the creek bed behind the house.

Pike's men fell one by one. Donovan took down Amos Parsons with a clean shot to the chest. Parsons reached for the knife in the scabbard at his waist, but his hand flopped in death halfway there.

Sterling's rifle barked, dropping another Coyote near the corral. Nate wondered if he'd had to kill his brother, Everett.

Scanning the yard, Nate saw bodies, blood, slats from a broken water barrel... but no sign of Pike.

Where is he?

Nate wanted him. Wanted him dead.

Keeping low, he sprinted toward the half-framed barn; they'd raised four walls, the beginnings of a loft above a dirt floor. He rose from his crouch, cutting behind the corral fence. The barn loomed ahead, half-shadowed.

Then, a bullet punched into the barn wall, inches from Nate's head. He flinched as splinters rained down, then swung out and fired. One outlaw dropped, clutching his side, as another ducked behind the water trough and returned fire.

Shoulder burning from the recoil, Nate moved along the barn's edge, trying to draw fire away from the house.

Faith had made it to the porch; she crouched low, reloading with practiced hands. She looked up, caught his eye, and nodded once.

They were in this together. He drew a breath of thankfulness. She wouldn't let anyone pass to get through the door.

He pressed forward, slipping between the barn and the corral. Every step felt like a lifetime. He felt the weight of it all pressing down. Travis's bruised face, the memory of Faith's kiss still lingering on his lips.

He hadn't meant for that to happen. Not then. Not like that.

But he didn't regret it.

Another shot rang out, and Nate dropped to one knee, returning fire. The man behind the trough slumped forward, motionless.

Nate reached the side door of the barn, kicked it open—and froze.

Pike stood in the middle of the straw-covered floor, framed by shafts of sunlight streaming between the unfinished beams above, ghostly fingers of light slicing down. He looked around, wild-eyed, torn coat hanging open like a flayed hide, blood dripping steadily from one sleeve. A deep gash split his brow, leaking a slow trickle of red down his temple and onto his collar.

But his stance was steady, coiled with purpose, his grip unshakable. One arm locked around Jed's collar like a vice; the other held a pistol against the boy's temple. He looked like a man with nothing left to lose, and that made him more dangerous than ever.

Jed's face was a mess. A fresh bruise bloomed across his cheek, lip split, one eye nearly swollen shut. His chest heaved with shallow, terrified breaths. He didn't cry. He didn't speak. He just looked at Nate like the scared little boy he was.

Nate's stomach dropped, cold and hard.

My son...

Pike smiled, slow and mocking. "Well, well... Look who finally showed up. It's your dear ol' daddy."

Nate stepped forward, gun raised, but his hands shook with the pounding of his heart. His vision narrowed to Jed's pale face, the black barrel of the pistol in Pike's hand. His mind raced. He felt sweat sliding down his back, the weight of every decision punching against his ribs.

Outside, Faith shouted something he couldn't make out. The fight was still raging. But here, in the barn, everything had narrowed to this moment.

Nate wanted Pike dead and buried, once and for all. Wanted vengeance for every wound the man had caused, seventeen years ago and now.

But not at the cost of losing Jed.

"Let him go, Pike." Nate stepped forward, voice trembling with restraint. "Only a coward would use a boy as a shield."

Pike's eyes gleamed with unholy fury, like a preacher seeing visions of hellfire. "You think I care what you think?" he snarled. "I came here to destroy you, Holt, to make you suffer like you made me."

He yanked Jed closer with a vicious jerk. The boy gasped, his breath catching on a sob. His legs shook as his feet scraped against the barn floor, searching for footing that wasn't there. Just a kid, caught in a war he never chose.

The very nightmare Etta had feared all these years, come true.

Nate's grip on the revolver tightened until the metal bit into his palm. "I said, *let him go.*"

Pike's bitter laugh echoed off the barn studs, a dry sound that chilled Nate's blood.

Jed whimpered; the raw, wounded sound sliced through Nate like a blade. The boy's knees buckled, but Pike held him firm, the pistol pressed so tight it left a pale mark on Jed's temple.

Nate's knuckles went white around the revolver. His heart was a war drum in his chest, fast and furious. The barn was too open—no cover, no angle, no chance to fire without risking Jed. Every breath felt like a countdown.

"I'll kill you," Nate said, voice shaking with fury. "I swear to God, if you hurt him..."

Pike's cruel smile widened calmly, like he'd already made peace with the devil. "You'll try—but shoot, and this boy dies with me."

"You want me to suffer?" Nate said. "Fine. But leave him out of it."

Pike tilted his head, eyes narrowing. "You'd trade yourself?"

"I would."

Jed's eyes widened. "No, Pa—"

"Quiet," Pike snapped, digging the pistol into Jed's cheekbone.

Jed flinched, his whole body taut with terror.

Nate, however, didn't flinch. Slowly, he lowered his Colt to his side, the gesture heavy with finality.

Pike hesitated. Then, with a violent shove, he hurled Jed forward.

The boy stumbled, legs folding beneath him, and hit the hard-packed ground. The *thud* of his knees on the straw-strewn dirt sounded painful. He lay there, gasping, arms curled protectively around his head.

I'm unarmed. Jed's still in danger, and I've got to find a way to keep Pike from ending everything here.

Nate stood, motionless, eyes locked on Pike, desperate for an answer. Only one word came to mind.

ZACHARY MCCRAE

Help!

Chapter Thirty

The barn seemed to hold its breath. The air shimmered with wheat chaff, catching the light in trembling motes that made everything feel unreal, like a dream. Only the rasp of Jed's shallow breathing broke the silence, mingling with shouts and gunfire in the distance.

What waited outside? Pike's gang? Help from Donovan or Sterling? Or were they all dead? Would Pike finally win?

Not as long as I have breath.

Nate's Colt hung at his side, heavy and useless. He'd lowered it to save his son, but now, he wasn't sure what he'd saved him from—or if he'd saved him at all. His heart thudded against his ribs, so loud, he wondered if Pike could hear it.

He didn't know how to get out of this. Not with Jed still on the ground, terrified to move. Not with Pike's rage simmering like a fuse held to a stick of dynamite. Nate's mind raced, grasping for a plan, a miracle, anything, but all he felt was the slow creep of dread, like the walls were closing in and time was running out.

Pike's gaze flicked between him and Jed, calculating. "You think you're clever, Holt?" he growled. "Looks like I win, after all. You're unarmed—or you *will* be, when you toss that Colt here."

For a split second, Nate entertained the idea of putting a bullet through Pike's chest. His fingers tightened around the grip of his Colt. *Just lift and shoot...*

"Don't even think about it, Holt." Pike cocked his pistol, the sound loud and ominous, as he pointed to Jed's head. "You may hit me, but I may hit the boy. Are you ready to risk his life?"

Nate swallowed hard. The Colt felt like lead in his hand. He tossed it at Pike's feet, the metal thumping against the dirt floor like a death knell. Fear hammered in his chest, but his voice came out steady like he was borrowing calm from somewhere.

"What's your plan here, Pike? So, you kill me. You get revenge. What then? Sooner or later, someone will catch up to you, and this time, no judge will let you escape the gallows."

"Shut up, Holt!"

Nate took a slow step forward, hands open, palms visible. "You were something once," he said coaxingly. "You rode like the devil was behind you. Folks whispered your name like it meant something. They feared you. But now? Look at you—old and tired, holding a gun to a boy's head because you've got nothing left. You and the Coyote Clan were legends. *Once*."

Pike stepped forward, kicking the Colt out of reach. "Legend?" he spat. "I rotted in a cell while you played lawman. You had a son. A wife. A *life*. I had rats and iron bars."

"You're tired, Pike," Nate kept talking as if the outlaw hadn't spoken. "You've been obsessed with revenge for so long, you forgot what it feels like to be alive."

A muscle jumped beneath Pike's stubbled cheek. "Don't you dare—"

"You're not the man you were anymore," Nate continued inexorably. "You're just a shadow, limping along, clinging to old grudges. You think killing me will bring it all back?"

Scowling, Pike stalked forward. "You think you're better than me?"

"No," Nate replied, "but at least I'm fighting for something. You just want to burn it all down."

Pike's hand trembled on the pistol. Fury and grief tangled together in his glassy eyes. "You think I wanted this?" he hissed. "That I wanted to live on this side of the law? Ma worked a saloon in a tiny Texas town so far off the road, the sun couldn't find it. Pa was a drifter who showed up just long enough to leave her with another mouth to feed!"

Nate shook his head, realizing he was finally getting answers to his questions about why men like Pike wanted to hurt others.

"Know what it's like to be beaten more than you get fed?" Pike scoffed. "Of *course* you don't. Early on, I learned that the weak don't survive without preying on the *weaker*. I killed my first man when I was just fourteen." Pike's face glowed maniacal satisfaction, like the deed was something to be proud of. "An old rancher who wouldn't pay for protection from the gang I rode with. Before long, I was *leading* that gang—me! Owen Pike! What do you think about that, Holt?"

"I think you don't know how to stop."

Pike lunged, his revolver clattering to the ground.

Nate braced himself as the outlaw slammed into him, fists flying. Nate staggered back, catching a blow to the jaw that flashed stars in front of his eyes. They grappled, boots scraping through the straw scattered on the floor, fists thudding into flesh.

Pike's rage made him reckless; he was strong, but sloppy and weak from years in prison.

Nate twisted, trying to throw him off, but Pike drove a knee into his side, and they crashed into a hay bale. Nate's breath left him in a grunt, and he glanced down to see Jed, still frozen with terror.

"Jed!" Nate shouted, voice raw. "Run!"

A second later, Pike slammed Nate against a beam, forearm pressed to his throat. "You think you can save him?" he spat. "You can't save anyone!"

Nate clawed at Pike's arm, gasping. "Jed! Go! R-run!"

But Jed cowered on the floor, trembling, tears streaking his dirt-smeared face.

Nate's heart broke. *I failed. I gambled everything on words and lost.* The world around him faded as Pike pressed his throat, cutting off his air. Death taunted him, beckoning him closer...

A shot rang out.

Sharp. Final.

The report boomed through the half-finished loft like thunder. Birds scattered from the rafters in a flurry of wings. The acrid scent of gunpowder rose to mingle with the sweet rot of hay and the sharp scent of blood.

Pike jerked, eyes widening in shock. His grip on Nate's throat loosened. Crimson bloomed across the chest of his linen shirt as he staggered back, mouth gaping in a soundless gasp, and collapsed in the dirt.

His fingers twitched convulsively, then lay still. A dark pool spread beneath him, soaking into the straw.

Nate's knees hit the ground as he gasped—fresh, throat-aching breath rasping its way back into his lungs—then looked up slowly.

Faith stood in the open door. Her arms trembled violently, the revolver still tight in her hand. Her lips parted, but no sound came. Her eyes stayed locked on Pike's chest, as if willing it to rise again.

"I didn't mean to," she whispered finally, the words barely audible. "He was hurting you, and I wanted... I couldn't..."

Wordlessly, Nate turned toward her and nodded once, slowly, in understanding. Then, he staggered over to Jed and pulled the boy into his arms. He wished he could've shielded his son from all the world's ugliness, but it was too late. The boy had seen the gunshot, the blood... everything.

Jed clutched Nate's shirt, burying his face against his pa's chest, and sobbed.

Nate held him tightly. "It's over," he murmured. "It's over, Jed. Pike's gone."

Faith's breaths came in shallow bursts. "I didn't want this," she rasped, as though to herself.

Nate looked at her, then at Pike's body. Remembering the outlaw's troubled life filled him with a heavy weight. *Such a waste.* "None of us did," he replied, "but you stopped him. You saved us."

Jed's sobs quieted, replaced by hiccuping breaths.

Nate stroked his hair. "We're going to be okay," he said, more firmly now. "We'll clean this up. We'll get through it."

Then, unable to help himself, he squeezed Jed so tightly that the boy gasped as joy flooded his heart. "We're alive, Jed!"

Chapter Thirty-One

Faith's ears rang. Her arms trembled.

The revolver hung heavy in her numb hands, as though molded to her fingers.

Pike's body lay crumpled on the straw, twisted in a way that made her stomach lurch. Blood seeped outward in slow, dark petals. His mouth was open, as though to utter another threat or, perhaps, a plea.

But he wouldn't speak again. Not ever.

Faith couldn't move. Her gun was still pointed at his chest, though the bullet had already done its work. Her heart thudded against her ribs like it was trying to escape.

"I shot him," she whispered.

It wasn't a question. It wasn't even a confession. It was just a painful truth.

The barn was silent except for the soft, broken sobs of a child. Faith stood frozen, willing Pike's chest to rise, to undo what had just happened.

"I didn't mean to," she whispered, though the words felt useless. "He was hurting you, and I wanted... I couldn't..."

Her voice sounded like it belonged to someone else. Her limbs were heavy, her breath shallow.

I didn't want this.

She didn't realize she'd spoken aloud until Nate replied, "None of us did, but you stopped him. You saved us."

Shaking, Jed clung to his pa. Nate held him close, murmuring, one hand cradling the boy's head, the other smeared with blood.

Faith's heart twisted. *He shouldn't have had to see that.*

"Faith," Nate said, voice rough. "You all right?"

She turned slowly, feeling like she was made of wet clay: soft, crumbling, barely holding together. She felt like an owl, staring out from wide, hollow eyes.

Blinking, she forced herself to answer. "I don't know."

Nate gently peeled Jed's arms from around his waist and murmured something she couldn't hear. Then, he stood and crossed the barn in three strides. He took the revolver from her hands, gently, as though disarming a child.

Her fingers didn't resist. They simply opened.

"I didn't mean to," she repeated.

"I know." Nate reached for her, pulling her into his broad, comforting arms.

She stiffened, unsure if she deserved comfort, unsure if she could accept it—but then, her body gave in, collapsing against him. As her forehead fell against his soft cotton shirt, she smelled blood, sweat, and oddly enough, pine needles.

She let herself cry then—silent, shaking sobs that felt like she'd held them in for years. Relief seeped through her body, slow and quiet, as she surrendered to the safety of Nate's embrace.

Dimly, Faith heard boots, and then a steady, familiar voice finally grabbed her attention.

"Faith? Nate?"

Relief flooded her. *Donovan!*

She couldn't force her voice to work, but thankfully, Nate shouted, "We're safe—it's over!"

The barn door creaked fully open, and Donovan stepped inside, silhouetted against the afternoon light. His eyes swept the scene quickly: Jed, sniffling, near where the stalls would go when they finished the barn; Faith, trembling in Nate's arms; Pike's motionless body, lying twisted in the straw.

"Land almighty!" Donovan muttered, stepping forward. "Pike..." He glanced at the body, then walked over to rest a steady hand on Jed's shoulder.

"I'm so glad you're safe, Jed," he said gently. "Lydia will be relieved to know you didn't get hurt." He turned to Faith and Nate. "We found Lydia trussed up like a Sunday hen to the clothesline. Pike managed to get here and grab Jed before she could hide in the cellar."

Jed nodded, his face streaked with tears. "I heard riders, so I locked Deck in the cabin so he wouldn't get hurt, but I couldn't help Miz Lydia—" His voice broke. "I t-tried!" he wailed.

"You did good," Nate assured him. "I couldn't ask for a braver son."

"He is, at that," Donovan agreed with a broad smile, then sobered. "We got the rest," he murmured to Nate. "Some tried to hole up near the creek. Two are dead, an' the other four are cuffed and headed for jail—tied 'em up myself. Sterling's brother is one of the four."

Faith's knees buckled, and Nate tightened his grip, steadying her. "Did you get all of 'em?" he asked.

Donovan nodded grimly. "They won't be coming back."

Faith exhaled, a sound halfway between a sob and a gasp. Pike was gone. The man who had twisted her life, who'd threatened and, likely, murdered Caleb. A man who had held the town in fear.

"He's really gone," she breathed, "but... I didn't want to kill him."

"I know," Donovan said gently, "but sometimes, that's the only way to get justice. Come tomorrow morning, Niobrara will get a fresh start."

Faith let herself believe he might just be right.

After everything they'd been through, it was finally over.

***

Faith followed Donovan and Nate into the afternoon light. Behind them, the barn door creaked shut, sealing away the chaos of the last hour.

Jed stood just outside, his small frame silhouetted against the golden sky. Uncertainty filled his wide eyes, and tears streaked his face.

Nate stood beside him, placing a steady hand on his shoulder. "Go on inside, son. We've got to go to town. You'll be safe with Miz Burke."

Jed nodded slowly, his eyes flicking toward the wagon parked near the well.

Faith followed the boy's gaze, and her stomach lurched.

Two long shapes lay in the wagon beneath a blood-soaked canvas. Behind the wagon, four outlaws stood in a line, hands bound with rope, guarded by the Holloway brothers. Their faces were hard, but their eyes betrayed fear. The fight had gone out of them.

Once Jed had gone inside, where the Deck's excited yips briefly lightened the somber mood, Nate turned to her. "As soon as we load Pike onto the wagon, I'm going into town. Talbot's going to hear about this. Why don't you stay here?"

Faith shook her head. "I'm going with you."

He gave her a crooked grin before rounding up their horses.

It didn't take long to ride into Niobrara. The wagon rolled into the town square, wheels groaning. Behind them, the four captive Coyotes rode, bound and bruised, eyes hollow.

Donovan and Sterling rode alongside while Nate cleared a path through the gathering crowd. Faith followed on horseback, Delilah plodding patiently along.

No one jeered. No one cheered. The silence, though, was heavy with the quiet hope of people who'd seen too much, but who now dared to dream they could live without fear.

Nate dismounted, footsteps calm but firm as he strode toward the jail.

Talbot stood on the front steps, arms crossed, jaw tight. His badge was notably absent, his holster empty. He looked like a man who knew the tide had turned against him.

Nate stepped forward. "It's over. Pike's dead. The Coyote Clan is finished."

Talbot's eyes flicked to the wagon, across the crowd, and back to Nate.

"You're under arrest," Nate continued steadily, "for obstruction of justice, aiding and abetting a fugitive, and dereliction of duty."

Talbot scoffed halfheartedly. "You think you can just take over? That slapping on a badge will make you sheriff?"

"I'm not wearing a badge," Nate said, "but someone has to do the job—and you stopped doing it a long time ago."

Talbot looked out over the square, at the faces of the people he'd failed. No one stepped forward to speak for him.

His shoulders sagged.

Nate reached into his coat and pulled out a pair of handcuffs. "Turn around."

Talbot hesitated, then did as he was told; the cuffs clanked with finality as Nate snapped them shut around his wrists. The crowd lingered as a member of the town council led Talbot away, murmurs rising like locusts through dry grass. No one protested. Instead, heads nodded. Shoulders straightened. A quiet ripple of approval moved through the square as Talbot went into the jail.

Donovan took charge, guiding the prisoners toward the jailhouse. The outlaws shuffled in silence, their eyes downcast. He opened the heavy door and ushered them inside, locking each cell with a final, echoing *clang* of iron—a sound the town hadn't heard in months.

Faith stood near the steps, watching Nate. He reached into his coat and pulled out his badge, the one Talbot had dishonored. He turned it over in his hand, then pinned it to his chest.

The silver star caught the late evening light, but Faith's pride shone brighter. Her throat tightened. It felt right.

"This town needs law. It needs protection, someone who won't turn away when things get rough." He took a deep breath and looked out over the crowd. "If you'll have me, I'd like to be sheriff again."

The crowd cheered.

Nate looked up, meeting Faith's gaze.

She nodded once. "You earned it," she said. "What happens now?" she asked as the people of Niobrara rushed forward to congratulate their new sheriff.

"We rebuild."

Someone jostled Faith to the side, but she didn't mind. Nate had earned this moment of glory.

Sheriff Nate Holt. It sounds just right.

Chapter Thirty-Two

The mornings had grown softer, touched with the crisp breath of autumn. The frantic days of survival had slowed, replaced by the steady rhythm of rebuilding. Faith felt it in her bones, the way the air no longer smelled of smoke and fear, but pine and damp earth.

It felt like weeks since they'd tried to ambush Pike and the Coyote Clan. Years since she'd shot and killed Owen Pike, earning the reward for his capture.

"A reward?" she'd asked when Nate brought the telegraph from a US Marshal in Yuma. "I don't want it." She still woke drenched in fear from reliving that gunshot in her nightmares. She wanted no reminders.

"Well," Nate had drawled, his eyes twinkling, "what am I supposed to do with it?"

"Give it to June and Travis. After all, Pike did murder their father."

"He had Amos Parsons kill Barrett," Nate had corrected, "but I reckon they'd be glad to have it."

Thankfully, despite his ordeal, Doc had declared that, with time and rest, Travis would make a full recovery. While they'd ridden to confront Sheriff Talbot, the McCall brothers had rescued Travis from hiding and taken him to Faith's ranch.

Travis breathed more easily now, the bruises on his cheeks fading into yellow-green. June rarely left his side. Sometimes, Faith lingered in the doorway, watching the two with mingled admiration and guilt.

If I had offered Pike my ranch earlier, he might never have taken Travis.

While Travis healed, other changes took place. The Burkes had asked to build a small cabin in the north field of Faith's ranch. After all they'd endured for her, Faith couldn't refuse. The general store wouldn't be opening anytime soon, not after the vandalism at the Harvest Festival.

Lydia had taken over Faith's kitchen, chopping onions with such fury that Faith laughed out loud, startling herself. Lydia cooked like she was feeding an army, and maybe she was—that many people had come to help Faith rebuild.

Donovan had begun to build a small shanty with Sterling's help, the two working in companionable silence, passing nails and boards like old friends. Faith watched them from the garden, her hands deep in the soil, planting winter greens. The land had been hard won, but it was hers.

Caleb would be proud.

Oddly, Gideon Hart had vanished; word was, the railroad had changed their plans. No more forced evictions. Hart had been seen leaving town on the day of the ambush, and as long as he didn't come back, Faith didn't care.

To her surprise, whenever his duties as sheriff allowed it, Nate showed up to help. He didn't say why, just kept coming—at dawn, with a hammer slung over his shoulder, or at dusk, with a bundle of kindling and a half-smile. Often, he brought Jed and Deck along, knowing how much she enjoyed the young boy's chatter and laughter.

Twice, he'd handed her a paper sack of cornmeal, making her blush at the reminder of the first time they'd met.

One afternoon, the sky had turned the color of pewter, heavy with the promise of rain that never came. Faith knelt beside the chicken coop, hammer in hand, her hair tied back with a strip of linen and sleeves rolled to the elbows. Her fingers were raw, her nails rimmed with soil, but she didn't mind. It felt good to concentrate on simple, honest work again.

Nate was nearby, sawing planks with steady precision. His shirt clung to his back, damp with sweat, and his jaw was set in that way that meant he was thinking—too much, probably. Faith caught him glancing at her again and again. She tried to ignore it, but her cheeks flushed despite herself.

"What?" she demanded finally, brushing a strand of hair from her cheek, worried she had dirt or chicken muck smeared across her face.

He laid the saw down and walked toward her slowly. His eyes were soft, uncertain, but determined.

"I've been trying to find the right time," he said.

Faith straightened, heart thudding. "For what?"

He reached out, his fingers grazing hers, calloused and warm. "To tell you that I'm in love with you."

Faith blinked. "You're..."

"I didn't mean for it to happen," he said quickly. "After Etta... Well, I figured I wouldn't love again. I didn't come here for that, though. I came because I wanted to help—but somewhere between the day you tossed cornmeal all over me and the day you saved my boy from Pike... Well, I guess my heart just—"

Before he could finish, Faith closed the space between them, pulled his face down to hers, and kissed him. Her hands cupped his chin, rough with stubble, and leathery cheeks. The world narrowed to the space between them, the warmth of his skin, the scent of pine and sweat, the soft clucking of chickens in the background.

When she pulled back, the taste of him lingered on her lips. "I love you too."

Nate's lips curved in a smile that made her feel like life was beginning again.

For a while after that, they just stood there, the sky still threatening rain. The chickens pecked at the dirt like nothing had changed—and maybe it hadn't, in their world.

But something had shifted inside Faith. With Nate's arms around her waist, she leaned back against his broad chest. She reached for his hand, lacing her fingers through his. His grip was firm, reassuring.

"Should we have a wedding?" she asked softly.

"I think that's a right smart idea. Will you marry me, Faith Shaw?"

In that moment, beneath the pewter sky, surrounded by the quiet sounds of her ranch, Faith could think of only one answer.

Chapter Thirty-Three

The golden sun rose over Niobrara like it had something to prove, spilling generous light across rooftops and cottonwoods. Nate stood at the edge of the town square, watching the final touches go up for their special day: white bunting strung between porch posts, wildflowers tucked into jars, tables groaning under the weight of Lydia's fine cooking for the feast to come.

My wedding day.

He hadn't slept much.

Not from nerves, exactly. More like awe, the kind that kept a man awake in anticipation of a dream coming true. He recalled his wedding to Etta, so long ago, it felt like it'd happened to someone else.

I was a different person. This time around, I'll be a better person because of Faith and Jed.

"Nate!" Donovan's voice cut through the hum of preparations. "What are you doing out here? Go get that suit and tie on before Lydia sees you aren't dressed yet and has a conniption."

"Too late." From the corner of his eye, Nate watched Lydia bustle toward them, apron flapping, hands full of peach pies.

"Nate Holt! You put on that suit I ironed for you!" she barked. "Donovan, why didn't you help him?"

"I tried," Donovan said, backing away quickly; obviously, he knew better than to cross his wife when she was in a mood.

Nate raised his hands in surrender. "I'm going, right this second, I swear."

Lydia narrowed her eyes. "You have twenty minutes. If you're not in that suit, I will personally drag you into it."

Chuckling, Nate ran toward the boarding house, heart thudding in a musical rhythm.

The blue serge suit had been Donovan's second best, tailored to Nate's somewhat leaner, taller form by Lydia with several muttered curses and a lot of pins. It fit well enough, though a few inches of ankle peeked out beneath the hem of the trousers.

Nate stared at himself in the mirror, tugging at the collar, wondering if Faith would laugh when she saw him. He almost hoped she did; it might make him feel more like himself.

Outside the window, he could see the town gathering. Children darted between tables, chasing one another. Old men leaned on canes, swapping stories about weddings they'd seen—and ones they'd run from. Women bustled around, putting together a feast to celebrate the bride and groom. The Niobrara River shimmered in the distance, calm for once, like it, too, had decided to settle down.

It was a fine day for a wedding.

With a nervous tug at his tie, Nate grabbed his hat, checked his beard for crumbs, and hurried out the door. He stepped off the boarding house porch just as a fiddle and banjo struck up a bright, bold tune.

Faith had wanted to hold the ceremony in the new bandstand in the town square. "So all our friends can be there," she'd said as they planned the celebration.

The bandstand, freshly painted in soft white, with garlands of ivy and yellow ribbon twining around its posts, stood in the center of town. The wooden floor still smelled of sawdust and sun-warmed pine, and the railings gleamed where Royce had polished them the night before. Around it, the townsfolk had gathered, many seated on mismatched chairs borrowed from porches and parlors, others standing shoulder to shoulder, craning their necks for a better view. There were rocking chairs with worn cushions, kitchen stools, a velvet parlor seat with one leg shorter than the rest, and even a hay bale draped in a quilt. It was a patchwork of their community, stitched together by those who'd come to witness Faith and Nate's vows.

June sat beside Travis, her hand resting lightly on his arm, her eyes shining. She'd braided her hair with bits of ribbon and wore a brooch shaped like a sparrow, Faith's favorite bird. Old Widow Nelson sat in a wicker chair with a cushion embroidered decades ago, chewing a wad of snuff, grinning toothlessly. No doubt, she'd tell everyone at dinner how she'd caught the Coyote Clan singlehandedly.

Jed leaned against the railing of the general store's porch, arms crossed, his hat tipped back to catch the breeze. Beside him, Deck perched on the edge of a barrel, tongue lolling as his stumpy tail waved. Nate had sat Jed down for a long talk after asking Faith to marry him, worried the boy might feel resentful. Happily, Jed liked Faith and made no objections at all—except for one request.

"Pa? When you and Miz Shaw get married, will she live at our ranch?"

"Yes, that's what we plan."

"Do you think you and Mr. Burke could build me a bedroom? That parlor floor's getting kinda hard."

Just remembering his son's ready acceptance of Faith added to Nate's joy as he hurried to take his place beside Royce, his best man, and a visiting preacher from Miner's Glen.

The preacher cleared his throat, and the crowd settled. Every eye turned to watch as Faith stepped out of the boarding house, a vision in pale pink and ivory lace. A breeze stirred the wildflowers in her auburn hair, lifting the hem of her dress just enough to reveal the worn boots she'd stubbornly refused to trade for finer slippers.

Nate's breath caught as she approached. Her steady gaze met his, and the world narrowed to the space between them.

Royce gave a subtle nod, his hands clasped behind his back. The preacher began to speak, his warm voice threading through the hushed anticipation.

Faith had wanted everyone there, and they were—every mismatched chair, every weathered face, every friend who'd helped them through the struggles of the last few months. As Nate reached for her hand, the sun broke through the clouds, casting golden light over the square, as if blessing the day itself.

Eyes shining, Faith whispered, "You're staring."

"I'm allowed," he whispered back and squeezed her hand. "You're mine now."

"Well, almost," she teased.

The ceremony was short, Preacher Eli's voice steady as he spoke about the events leading up to the special day. "We are here to witness the joyful union of Faith Shaw and Nate Holt. We've gathered to celebrate, not just love, but survival. Not just hope, but the choice to persevere and begin life anew."

Nate held Faith's work-roughened palms against his as the words wrapped around them like a promise.

When Preacher Eli said, "You may kiss the bride," Faith almost beat him to the moment.

The crowd erupted in cheers and applause, someone whistling loud enough to startle the chickens behind the Gold

Dust. The fiddle and banjo burst out in a sprightly tune as Nate led Faith down the steps of the bandstand. Friends rushed forward with hugs and congratulations.

The feast spilled into the afternoon. Tables were filled with roast chicken, cornbread, peach pies, jugs of lemonade and cider. The hard-packed street became a dance floor, stomped by couples as they swung into square dances and jigs.

Nate sat beside Faith, their hands clasped, watching the townsfolk celebrate like they'd been waiting years for a reason to be happy again.

Donovan raised a glass. "To second chances."

"To beginning again," Lydia added.

Nate had eyes only for his bride. Faith leaned against him, pink-cheeked, green eyes shining.

"To love," he whispered for her ears only, "and maybe a busted sack of cornmeal."

Faith blushed.

Epilogue

One year later

The sun had dipped low behind the cottonwoods, casting golden streaks across the tablecloth. They'd dragged three planks together under the old oak behind Nate's house. The air smelled of grilled meat, sweet corn, and the faint tang of woodsmoke. Laughter rose and fell like music.

Nate sat back in his chair, letting it all wash over him. He hadn't known this kind of peace in years. Not really. Not the kind that settled in your bones and made you believe you'd earned it.

Travis Rivers was telling a story, something about a mule refusing to cross a creek, as Jed wheezed with laughter, elbowing June, who rolled her eyes but smiled anyway. Donovan and Lydia sat close, fingers laced, her head resting on his shoulder. Royce had brought a bottle of some fancy, expensive liquor and was pouring it with exaggerated flair. Faith giggled like a little girl.

Faith. My Faith.

She was glowing tonight, not just from the firelight, but something deeper. Nate watched her as she leaned into the conversation, her eyes bright, her hand resting absently on her stomach.

She hadn't said it yet. But he knew.

Nate had known since she'd paused in the garden that morning, one hand on her belly, the other brushing soil from a carrot. She'd looked at him then, green eyes wide and soft, and he'd felt the world tilt.

He'd taken her gently in his arms and pulled her close. "I feel like you might have something to tell me."

Faith had nodded, her face pressed to his chest. "How would you like to be a papa again?"

"I can't think of anything I'd like more," he'd answered, then felt the old familiar dread. "Maybe it's time I hung up my guns a—"

"You'll do no such thing!" Faith's green eyes had flashed with a fire he'd come to know well. "You're the best sheriff Niobrara has ever had, and our baby will be proud of his papa."

Nate had laughed. "What if she's a girl?"

Hands on her hips, Faith had answered staunchly, "She'll be even prouder."

Now, as the laughter died down and Royce raised his glass for a toast, Nate felt a hush settle. The kind that comes before something important.

"To family," the older man said, voice thick with an emotion he rarely showed. "The kind you're born into, the ones you find, and those you fight for—the kind you keep."

Faith stood, her fingers curled around her glass, firelight catching tints of lighter red in her hair. "I'd like to say something," she began, clearing her throat, "and I reckon it's best said plain. We want everyone to know."

The table quieted. Even the cicadas out in the garden seemed to sense that something significant was coming.

"I'm with child."

For a heartbeat, the world held still.

Then, June let out a squeal so sharp it startled Sebastian, who hissed and shot off to join the rest of the barn cats. Royce spilled his drink as Lydia gasped and clapped her hands over her mouth. Donovan jumped up and hugged Faith hard; then, seeming to realize he might've squeezed her a little *too* hard, he backed away, flustered.

Slapping his knee, Travis hollered, "Well, I'll be! That's the best news I've heard in a long time! Does that mean I get to be an honorary uncle?"

Jed just sat there, stunned, before breaking into a smile that crinkled his eyes. "Does this mean I'm gonna be a big brother?"

"It does, indeed," Faith told him, reaching out to clasp his hand. At thirteen, Jed had grown taller than his stepmother, but was still a boy at heart.

Jed's grin stretched so wide, his face looked like to split, his cheeks flushed with excitement. Faith looked at him with a tenderness that made Nate's chest ache.

"Deck can belong to him, too," Jed decided, reaching down to pat the mutt, who was never far from his feet. Deck leaned into his touch, tail thumping against the ground like a steady heartbeat.

"What if it's a *her*?" June teased, her tone light, but she searched his face with careful eyes.

Jed paused, hand resting on Deck's scruff. His grin faltered for breath, then returned, gentler now. "Then *she* can belong to Deck," he declared, voice thick with the fragile hope of imagining a future not yet written and unspoken emotion: nervous anticipation, tempered with tentative affection—maybe even love. "Reckon a sister might take some getting used to, though."

Travis whooped again. "Forget it, Jed—you'll never get used to a sister!"

After all the hugs and congratulations, they fell to suggesting names for the baby. Royce, tipsy on his fancy liquor, speculated over the origin of Faith's condition; fortunately, before his comments could cross the line from suggestive to outright risqué, Lydia snapped her fingers in front of his nose, eyeing Jed significantly.

Nate didn't care. He just held Faith's hand and basked in the love surrounding him. Royce had been right; these people really were his newfound family.

Jed, who'd come to him filled with anger because of Etta's fear, now glowed with anticipation of the joys to come.

Travis and June, who'd survived their father's death, had come out stronger. Not long after Nate and Faith's wedding, Travis had joined Nate as a deputy, while June had moved into town to teach at Niobrara's growing school.

Donovan and Lydia, who'd watched their dreams reduced to ruins, had built something from the ashes. The general store might be gone, but now, they had a new home. After marrying Nate, Faith had given the Burkes her ranch. It had only made sense, seeing as Donovan knew the land and livestock just as well as Faith—and when the old bull, Brutus, came wandering up one day, it had felt like the perfect omen.

Royce, who'd been with them through it all, had found a new friend in Sterling Pierce; once Pierce finished his time in prison, he'd have a home at the Gold Dust.

And Faith—his Faith—who'd seen the broken man Nate had been and loved the man he'd become, stayed by his side.

As the night wore on, stories flowed as they recounted events from the past year: the nightmares that haunted them, the scars that didn't fade, the days when grief sat heavy, and the lessons they'd learned. They talked about them together, knowing their family circled them in love—not despite their trials, but *because* of them.

Later, when the fire had burned down and stars glittered overhead, Nate found himself standing alone by the corral fence, looking up at the stars. He thought about the child growing inside Faith, about the world he wanted to build for Jed and the baby.

Then, Faith joined him, curling into his side, and her hand found his. She squeezed gently, grounding him in the present. "It's getting late. Aren't you coming in?"

As leaves rustled, an owl called in the distance. Nate closed his eyes, letting peace sink into his bones. "Just taking a moment to enjoy the night. I've come a long way—from a man who couldn't sleep through the night, flinched at kindness, and didn't believe he deserved love. Now, I'm surrounded by it."

And at that moment, Nate realized that his once-bitter heart finally believed that this love, this peace, would last.

THE END

Also by Zachary McCrae

Thanks for ridin' along with **"Once a Lawman"**!

If it hit the mark for you, you can find more of my stories right here:

https://go.zacharymccrae.com/bc-authorpage

Thank you kindly!